TRUTH AND
LIES

>> a MIKE & RIEL MYSTERY >>>

TRUTH AND LIES

NORAH McCLINTOCK

darbycreek

MINNEAPOLIS

First U.S. edition published in 2014 by Lerner Publishing Group, Inc.

Darby Creek
A division of Lerner Publishing Group, Inc.
241 First Avenue North
Minneapolis, MN 55401 U.S.A.

For reading levels and more information, look up this title at
www.lernerbooks.com.

Front cover: © Hemera/Thinkstock.

Main body text set in Janson Text LT Std 11.5/15
Typeface provided by Adobe Systems.

Library of Congress Cataloging-in-Publication Data

McClintock, Norah.
    Truth and lies / by Norah McClintock.
        p.   cm. — (Mike & Riel ; #2)
    Originally published by Scholastic Canada, 2004.
    Summary: Mike's lies are spinning out of control and now he's the
    number-one suspect in a murder. Okay, so he can't explain his bruised and
    skinned knuckles, and he can't explain why he was spotted near the park
    where Robbie was killed. But if Mike really is innocent, then why doesn't
    his alibi check out? And why are the police so sure that he's guilty?
        ISBN 978–1–4677–2606–1 (lib. bdg. : alk. paper)
        ISBN 978–1–4677–2614–6 (eBook)
    [1. Mystery and detective stories. 2. Foster home care—Fiction.] I.
Title.
PZ7.M478414184Tr 2014
[Fic]—dc23   2013017549

Manufactured in the United States of America
1 – SB – 12/31/13

CHAPTER ONE

Riel was standing in the kitchen in his sock feet, frowning, when I came down to breakfast. He glanced up from the newspaper. His already grim expression deepened.

"What happened to you?" he said. He was looking at my hands.

Jeez. I had to fight the urge to hide them behind my back or stuff them into my pockets. My main thought: He knows. He knows, and now I'm in for it—the third degree.

Stay calm, I told myself. *Admit nothing. Question everything.*

"What do you mean?" I said. I pitched my voice lower to compensate for the squeak that always creeps into it when I get nervous.

He was still staring at my hands. "Have you been fighting, Mike?"

I glanced at my knuckles. They were skinned in a few places and bruised in others. I forced a smile. "I was just horsing around with Sal," I said. That's what guys did, right? They horsed around. Stupid stuff.

"Yeah? How come I didn't notice that last night?"

"Maybe because you were marking papers right through supper." Riel had got home late, after I'd already cleared away my dishes, and he had worked while he ate. He'd dropped mustard on some kid's essay and then went nuts trying to get it off—like the kid would even notice, let alone care. So maybe he hadn't looked at my hands.

He pondered my answer for a moment and must have accepted it because he said, "You're running late." He sounded—what?—grumpy? Riel was a nice enough guy when he was relaxed—like on Friday nights when he didn't have to worry about prepping classes for the next day and made it a rule never to mark essays and tests. Or on Saturday nights if he was going out with Susan or if Susan came over for dinner. But on weekday mornings, forget it. On weekday mornings he was like some kind of manic efficiency expert, fussing and fretting if everything didn't run precisely according to schedule. *His* schedule. All that was missing was a stopwatch around his neck.

I checked the clock over the kitchen table.

"We've got plenty of time," I said. But Riel's idea of being on time was showing up fifteen minutes early, whereas I figured I was in the clear if the bell was still ringing when I dashed through the door to homeroom.

Riel dropped a couple of slices of whole grain bread into the toaster. Bread packed with little seeds. It was the only kind of bread he ever bought. Say Wonder Bread to him and he was ready to cross himself, like good old white bread was some kind of sin.

"Was it my imagination," he said, "or did I hear you wandering around down here pretty late last night?"

I yanked open the fridge door—it blocked Riel's view of me—and ducked to look inside. The fridge air cooled my hot face. I pulled out a carton of milk. *Organic* milk, what else?

"I had trouble sleeping," I said. That part was true. I reached for a glass in the cupboard, focusing my whole attention on it, like getting hold of that glass and not dropping it was the most important thing in the world. "I came downstairs to get something to drink."

Riel didn't say anything. I poured my milk before I dared a glance at him. He was studying the newspaper that he had spread out on the kitchen counter.

"Big story?" I said.

He shook his head. "No story," he said. "Not in the paper yet, anyway. I heard it on the radio."

"Heard what?"

"You know a kid named Ducharme?" he said.

There was a Ducharme who sat near the front of my math class. A guy who carried a calculator in his shirt pocket. He was that kind of guy, always wearing shirts that had pockets in them. "Robbie Ducharme?" I said.

"Radio said Robert." The toast popped up. Riel dropped both slices onto a plate and set it in front of me. "But, yeah, Robbie. You know him?"

"Robbie Ducharme's in my math class." Then, maybe because I'm never too swift in the morning, because it took time for it to sink in, I said, "He made the radio? How come?"

"He's dead," Riel said. There was that tone in his voice again. Not grumpy, I decided. More like angry. Even more like furious.

"Dead?" I said. "Of what?"

"All I know is what I heard on the radio." I got the feeling that this was something else that was bugging Riel. Now that he was "just" a teacher, he didn't have the inside track. He had to rely on the same sources as everyone else. "Seems he was kicked to death," Riel said. "Why would anyone want to kick a fifteen-year-old boy to death?"

Yeah, definitely angry.

"Is he in one of your classes?" I said.

He shook his head. "But I know the family."

Robbie Ducharme dead. Jeez. Robbie Ducharme with his calculator. Pulled a minimum ninety, ninety-five on every math test, even pop quizzes. Scored a lot of perfects too. I tried to remember who he hung out with, but came up blank. The truth was, I didn't pay much attention to Robbie Ducharme if I could help it, and believe me, I went out of my way to help it. Robbie and I weren't in the same league, let alone the same club.

"I'm sure the cops will figure it out," I said. Which, maybe they would and maybe they wouldn't. In the movies, they always nailed it. In real life . . . well, I knew the stats, especially now that I was living with Riel. The homicide clearance rate in Toronto was down. The cops made arrests in three out of four cases, if they were lucky. Some cases they never closed. But that wasn't why I'd said it. Mostly I had said it because of the look on Riel's face, the one he always had when he heard about the big cases on the news. Back before he had turned teacher, Riel had been a cop. Sometimes he acted like he was still on the job.

"You want peanut butter?" Riel said.

I shook my head. No way. Riel bought his peanut butter at the same health food store where he bought his seed-packed bread. The peanut butter was thick and hard to spread, and you had to stir it up with your knife first because there was always a gross layer of yellow-ish oil floating on top. Peanut oil, Riel said. Good for you—no additives, no fillers, no emulsifiers, whatever they were. No spreadability either. Maybe that's why he bought bread that was full of seeds—it didn't tear like good old soft sweet evil Wonder Bread.

Riel was staring at my knuckles again, studying them. It was probably eating at him that he hadn't taken a good look at my hands the night before.

"Looks like some serious horsing around," he said. "What's Sal look like? Am I going to hear from his parents?"

Give me a break! I made a face—he'd expect that from me—then shrugged, doing my best to play it easy.

"Sal looks fine," I said. "He ducked. I hit concrete."

There it was again, that look: *Does not compute.*

"With *both* fists?" Riel said.

"It was a one-two," I said. "I was pretty sure the second one would connect."

"With?" Disapproval was coming at me in waves now.

"With his shoulder. I already told you, we were just horsing around." Jeez. "We got any jam?"

"Some strawberry, I think," Riel said, moving toward the fridge.

"It's okay," I said, jumping up, showing some early morning energy that I didn't feel. "I'll get it."

"You've got five minutes," Riel said. He grabbed his mug of coffee and left the kitchen. Going to pack his briefcase, I figured. Going to make sure it contained his lesson plans and the papers he had marked and whatever diabolical assignment he was going to spring on his students next. "Five minutes and we're out of here. Got it?"

"Got it."

I waited until I was alone in the kitchen. Then I dumped the toast into the garbage can and poured my milk down the sink. My stomach felt as raw as my knuckles. Anything I ate was sure to come right back up again. *I should have stayed put last night*, I thought. *The way things worked out, I just should have stayed put.*

» » »

Anyone who hadn't heard about Robbie Ducharme when they arrived at school knew about him by the time the homeroom bell rang. While I was rooting around in my locker, I heard the buzz of Robbie's name up and down the corridor. *Did you hear about the Ducharme kid? He was kicked to death.* Some kids sounded like they couldn't believe it. Others sounded like they didn't really care. Me? I had problems of my own, like, *Where is my history textbook?*

I emptied the top shelf of my locker, textbook by binder by notebook. My history book wasn't there. It wasn't in the heap of stuff on the bottom of the locker either, although, hey, I did find my calculator, which would at least get Mr. Tran off my back. But my history book? Not there. I was pretty sure it wasn't at home either. Well, look on the bright side. I wasn't in Riel's history class anymore. They made me transfer out when he became my foster parent. If I'd still been in his class, I'd be in for trouble for sure because Riel was the kind of teacher who *always* noticed when kids didn't come prepared. He noticed because he *always* checked. And whenever he found kids who had come to class without their textbooks, he gave them extra assignments. He always said, "Maybe that will help you to come prepared next time."

My new teacher, Mr. Danos, wasn't such a stickler. But—and this is what always scared me, no matter whose class I was in—if Mr. Danos and Riel got talking in the staff lounge at lunch, and if Mr. Danos happened to mention that I had come to class without my textbook, Riel would make a mental note of that. And later, maybe over supper or maybe when I was cleaning up afterward, I'd get the lecture. *You should always be prepared, Mike. You should look after your things. You should take school seriously. You have to be responsible, Mike.* And he'd make me tear apart my room until I either found the book or proved that I had exhausted all possibilities. Then he'd make me promise to tear apart my locker the next day. And if I did that and still didn't produce the book, *blam*, I'd be hit with another lecture. *Your textbooks are your responsibility, Mike. They're expensive, you know. I hope you're not expecting me to pay for it.* And then, inevitably, *Have you been giving out your locker combination again, Mike? I thought we covered that. I thought we agreed that wouldn't happen anymore.* Jeez, Riel. He *told* you what to do, then he said, *That's what we agreed, right?*, like life in his house was one big happy democracy, like he wasn't really 100 percent in charge of what happened. I had to get my hands on that book by the end of the day or else. And I had just one more idea where it might be.

I slammed my locker shut and headed for homeroom. Robbie Ducharme's name was in the air all around me. I bet Robbie had never been noticed so much. For the whole day his name was whispered, spoken, exclaimed in hallways, in bathrooms and out in the schoolyard. *Did you hear what happened to Robbie Ducharme? Why would anyone do such a thing?* Why would anyone bother? The guy was a nobody. A nothing. Less than that—a negative number.

The cops came around. They stayed in the office, mostly. Probably asking about Robbie—who did he hang with? Did he have any troubles with anyone? Was he a scrapper? Later, I figured, they'd want to start talking to Robbie's teachers and to kids who had maybe known Robbie.

Mr. Tran, my math teacher, normally couldn't stand still for five seconds because he was always so jazzed about math, like all that stuff he was scribbling on the chalkboard added up to the secret of the universe. But today Mr. Tran was sitting at his desk, as hard and fixed as his chair. The only way you could tell he was breathing was that every now and again his chest would heave, like he was gasping for air. When the bell rang at the beginning of class, he got up and started to write on the board—another formula, every day one more useless line of code to learn. His usually square, careful writing got faster and wilder and scribblier and then, as he was drawing a line, slashing at the board to do it, the chalk snapped. Mr. Tran wheeled around, raised his hand, and threw the half piece of chalk that he was still holding. Threw it hard, so that Trevor Black, who sat near the back of the room and who hated math, had to duck. The chalk whizzed over his head and struck the back wall. Mr. Tran stared at the whitish spot where it had made contact. Stared, then turned and stalked from the room. Jeez.

At lunchtime I scoured the cafeteria for Vin. I found Sal instead. Vin Taglia is my best friend. I've hung out with him since kindergarten. Sal San Miguel is a newer friend, but solid just the same. When a guy has two friends like that, he hardly needs anything else.

"Hey," I said, sliding into a chair opposite Sal. He had a slice of pepperoni pizza on a paper plate in front of him. He hadn't touched it. I had a tuna sandwich on whole grain bread, and an apple. Riel never quit.

Sal's head bobbed up. He looked like he hadn't slept since the millennium began.

"You okay?" I said.

He nodded.

"You hear about Ducharme?"

Another nod. Jeez, you want to let a guy get a word in edgewise or what?

I took my sandwich out of the bag it was in and stared at it. Then I looked at the untouched pizza on Sal's plate, glistening with delicious but 100-percent-bad-for-you grease.

"You gonna eat that?" I said at last.

Sal shoved the plate across the table.

Well, okay.

» » »

I was halfway out one of the side exits after school, not thinking about anything special except maybe getting to my after-school job on time. I'd shoved open the door and was cruising through it and, believe me, I wasn't looking for her—why would I? In fact, I wasn't looking for anyone or anything in particular. But there she was, way over on the far side of the schoolyard. From where I was standing, if I held up a finger and positioned it so that it was right alongside her, way over there on the other side of the yard, she was tiny—no bigger than the nail on my index finger. But I spotted her right off. Even from so far away, she was achingly recognizable.

Jen.

I hadn't spoken to her since, well, since what had happened to my Uncle Billy. She'd been crying then and mostly what she had said was, "I'm so sorry."

Sorry about Billy.

Sorry about dumping me at what was the second-worst time in my life.

Sorry that she felt guilty about what she was doing.

Sometimes I thought that was the thing that had wrung the most tears out of her—that she felt guilty because she knew what she was doing was wrong. You couldn't say you loved somebody and then, when his—*my*—whole world was falling apart, just turn and walk out of his life. And for a while, that had given me hope. Jen was a nice person, a good person, the kind of person who, when she did something wrong and knew it, would sooner or later apologize. Would repent. Maybe would take me back.

But that hadn't happened.

She didn't even go to my school anymore. She had

transferred to a private girls' school uptown. A school where everyone was on the university track. Where a huge chunk of the students won scholarships. Where the ones who didn't have cars of their own had access to cars. Where the girls all had skin like velvet and bodies as slender as models'. It was like a different planet. But sometimes she dropped back into her old orbit to see her old friends. Well, some of her old friends.

I stood outside the school, watching her. She'd started going with a guy named Patrick just before she'd stopped being with me. Patrick, who also went to a private school. But I'd heard she wasn't seeing him anymore. I'd heard she wasn't doing so well at her new school. I'd heard that she wasn't so happy there. I thought maybe that was why she came back here from time to time. I thought—okay, so I hoped—maybe there was another reason too.

She was standing with another girl who lived on her street, a snot named Ashley who had been going to private school forever. Jen was talking to a couple of girls she had been close to when she went to my school. Ashley was looking off in the distance, making it clear that not only did she not know Jen's old friends, but that she didn't *want* to know them. I waited a minute, then a minute more, wondering if Jen would turn in my direction and, if she did, if she'd see me. But she never did.

» » »

I caught up with Vin at Gerrard Square. He was perched on the fence that ran along the west side of the parking lot. There was a girl with him. Cat—short for Catherine, which she thought was cool. So did Vin. When I saw her, I hesitated. But, hey, she was just a girl, and Vin was my best friend. *Was.* Lately I wasn't sure what was past tense and what was present.

Cat spotted me first and nodded in my direction. Vin turned. His face split with a smile.

"Hey, Mikey!"

Those two words and that big Vin smile made me feel warm all over. Everything was okay. A best friend is a best friend, right? Some things never change.

I walked over to Vin. He was still smiling, but Cat's expression was cool, like one of those fashion models you see on billboards or in bus shelter ads. Distant. Thinking about something—you didn't know what it was, but you knew it was more important than what was for supper and what was due for homework the next day. Her eyes—were they really golden or did they just look that way in the sun?—focused hard on me. On my eyes, then on my hands. Vin noticed and grinned.

"What've you been up to, Mike?" he asked. "Not getting yourself into trouble, I hope."

I couldn't help it, I felt my cheeks get warm. I shrugged and jammed my fists into the pockets of my jacket.

"It's nothing," I said.

"Sure," Vin said. I could tell he didn't believe me,

but for some reason he decided not to push it.

"I gotta go," Cat said, just like that. She leaned forward and planted a kiss and some bright red lipstick on Vin's cheek. Vin looked pleased—*Check it out, Mikey.* He glanced at me, maybe wanting to see if I looked jealous, and kept on grinning as Cat twirled and danced away from him, heading up the walkway over the railroad tracks. Vin stayed on the fence, an unlit cigarette dangling from his lips, watching her go.

"She's something, eh?" he said.

Cat was on the top of the walkway now, a thin girl with spiky hair, four studs in one ear, five in the other, an eyebrow ring, pale face, blood-red lips. Yeah, she was something.

"You hear about that kid, Ducharme?" I said.

Vin nodded. His head was still tilted up at the walkway. Cat was almost down the other side now. In a minute she would disappear from sight.

"What do you think happened?" I said.

"Huh?" He tore his eyes away from Cat and looked at me, surprised by the question. "What'd you say?"

"Robbie Ducharme. What do you think happened?"

Vin shrugged. "I guess someone didn't like him," he said. He took the unlit cigarette from his mouth and flicked it onto the road. "I gotta quit this," he said.

"You don't smoke, remember?" I said. Vin was allergic to cigarette smoke, but he walked around with an unlit cigarette in his mouth because he thought it made him look cool. The line he used was, "I'm trying to quit." A lot of girls think it's even cooler when you're trying to quit smoking, he had told me.

"What I mean is, I gotta quit trying to quit," Vin said. "These things aren't cheap, you know."

"In other words," I said, "Cat doesn't smoke."

Vin grinned.

"Correct," he said. "Doesn't smoke. Doesn't think smoking is cool. Her granny died of lung cancer. Her whole life is a smoke-free zone." He checked his watch, and then jumped down from the fence. "Hey, gotta go," he said.

"Wait." I knew I was going to sound like a real bonehead for asking this, but I had to. "You got my history book, by any chance?"

Vin at least had the decency to look embarrassed. "Yeah," he said. "Sorry about that. I forgot mine at home, and you know what Cop Boy is like when you show up in his class without a book."

Cop Boy. It's what Vin called Riel. "Can I have it back?"

Vin shrugged out of his backpack and rummaged through it. He handed me the book. I couldn't tell if it was my imagination or if the book really was more dog-eared than I remembered.

"Hey, Mike, I really do have to take off."

"A. J.?" I said and, I couldn't help it, I guess I sounded sort of ticked. A. J. Siropolous was a guy in twelfth grade. He was also the guy Vin had been spending time with. A. J. had a car and a lot of friends and always a line on a party. Vin was always saying, "Come on, Mikey, come with me. You'll have a great time, guaranteed." But Riel was always saying, "Done your homework yet?" And if the answer was yes, "Then show me." Riel took foster parenthood more seriously than Billy had taken guardianship. But then, what had I expected? I knew from the start that Riel was a serious guy. And if I *had* done my homework and if I could produce it and if the homework met Riel's expectations, which it didn't always, then the next question was, "What about your job? How's that going lately?" The job was something else Riel insisted on: a) that I have one; b) that I take it seriously; and c) that I put three-quarters of what I earned into a savings account.

"You're on your own, Mike," he'd say, not to be mean, although it always made me remember that Billy was gone now and that my mother was gone too, and had been for a lot longer. "You have to learn to look after yourself."

It turned out that looking after yourself was a very big deal with Riel. It turned out that his father had been killed in a work accident when Riel was just a kid, and his mother had died of breast cancer just as he was graduating high school. Riel had a younger sister, Beth. He'd looked after her for a few years, just like Billy had looked after me. Beth lived in Australia now, with a surfer. Riel never said so, but I could tell that he didn't approve by the look on his face and the tone of his voice when he mentioned the guy Beth lived with—a guy he always called *the surfer*, like he didn't have a name.

"A. J.'s got it together," Vin said. "If Cop Boy would let you off your leash for five minutes, you'd see. You'd like him." He shook his head. "I gotta tell you, Mike, you really picked the wrong guy!"

My belly started to tighten. For a moment I felt like I was going to throw up. I felt that way whenever I got really mad, which was a lot lately. Mad at Riel for being so serious all the time. Mad at Vin for riding Riel. Mad at Billy for leaving me in this situation in the first place.

"What was I supposed to do?" I said.

"There are lots of foster parents that are way more relaxed," Vin said.

"Maybe."

"Definitely. You know Gord Spinelli?"

A guy who hung around with A. J. sometimes. Maybe another of Vin's new best friends.

"He's in a foster home," Vin said. "Two foster parents—a couple. The guy works at the Ford plant in Oakville." Vin's dad worked there too. "The woman's a full-time mom. Looks after four foster kids, including Gord. She doesn't ride them about homework and go get a job and how about going out for every sport there is while you're at it."

Riel was as big on sports as he was on after-school jobs. He said sports kept kids out of trouble.

"The kids show up for school, they show up for supper, they show up for bed and do a few chores and she's cool," Vin said. "Relaxed. Not like Cop Boy."

"Stop calling him that," I said. "He's not a cop anymore."

"Okay." Vin looked at me like he was noticing all kinds of things about me he'd never noticed before, a halo maybe, and even some wings. "You're getting as straight as he is, Mikey. You know that?" He glanced at his watch. "Catch you later, okay? I gotta go." And off he went, up the incline of the walkway, over the tracks, down the other side. He didn't look back even once.

» » »

As soon as I opened the front door Riel shouted to me from the kitchen. I found him at the counter, slicing tomatoes for a salad. He waved me onto one of the stools opposite him and set his knife aside. Then he put both hands on the counter and leaned across to peer at me. "Tell me again about last night," he said.

I blinked. What was going on?

"What about last night?"

"You were here, right?" Riel said.

Jeez, I'd said I was, hadn't I? "Yeah, I was here."

"All night," he said, only it came out as another question.

"You saw me go up to my room," I said. I kept my hands out of sight, below the counter, just in case.

"I also heard you walking around in the middle of the night," he said.

"I was here." I looked Riel in the eyes. I knew him.

I knew he was watching for that. He had a reputation at school. If you didn't look straight at him when he asked why your homework wasn't done, he'd ask again and he'd say, *Look at me this time.* Cops. They like to believe they can tell a lie from the truth. They like to think the job has taught them that. So, okay, I locked eyes with Riel, mustered a little indignation, and said, "I already told you. I came down to get something to drink."

Riel peered into me, like he could read my soul.

"What's the matter?" I said. "Is something the matter?"

"There were kids in the park last night," Riel said. "In the park where they found Robbie Ducharme. People who live around there said they heard kids."

"There's always kids in that park," I said. "I used to—" I stopped abruptly.

"You used to what?"

There was no point in denying it.

"I used to hang around there myself." The three of us, me and Vin and Sal, we used to hang around the park all the time, at the far end, near the railroad tracks, away from all the houses. "Do they know what kids were there?"

Riel shook his head. "Just kids," he said. "Nobody that anyone could identify. And no kids have come forward."

I waited and watched as Riel picked up his knife. He started slicing tomatoes again, slowly, deliberately, paper-thin.

"There were kids in the park where the Ducharme kid was killed," Riel said. "And so far no one has come forward to say they saw anything. That make sense to you?"

CHAPTER TWO

"Hey," Sal said. He fell back against the brick wall and slid down it until he was squatting next to me. The roughness of the brick probably chewed up the back of his jacket, but he didn't seem to care.

"Hey," I said.

Silence. I glanced over at Sal. He was looking down at the ground.

"You okay?" I said.

Nothing for a moment. Then, "So, where's Vin at?"

As if I had any idea. I looked out across the schoolyard to see if I could spot him, but no. There were knots of girls here and there, clusters of guys under the basketball hoops, and Riel, in a black T-shirt and black jeans, supervising a softball practice. He was a first-class coach, the way some guys talked.

"You and him had a fight?" Sal asked.

"What, me and Vin?" I shook my head. It would have

been easier if that's what it was. I would have understood it—Vin isn't around because he's mad at me. But that wasn't it. "It's that girl he's seeing," I said. "Cat." A girl who liked a certain kind of guy, the kind of guy that Vin was all of a sudden interested in being.

"No!" someone yelled.

I turned and looked. It was pure reflex.

Over by one of the entrances to the school I saw two girls—Lisa and Voula. They were trying to back away from some man. Voula was having more success. The man grabbed Lisa by the arm and was holding tight.

"Let me go," Lisa said. She said it the way some girls say it to guys who are trying stuff, except she sounded scared.

"But you know him," the man said.

Lisa squirmed. Voula looked around, her eyes panicky. She seemed to be searching for a teacher or someone—anyone—who could help Lisa. She was kind of cute, but that wasn't what got my interest. The main thing about Voula was that she was an old friend of Jen's. I'd asked her once for Jen's cell phone number, but she hadn't given it to me. Maybe . . .

I nudged Sal. Then I stood up and yanked him to his feet.

"Just tell me you know him," the man said to Lisa.

"Yeah, okay," she said. She had stopped struggling, but she was watching the man intently. She was so still that I guessed she was trying to fake the man out so he'd loosen his hold a little and she could break free. Then there it was, the jerk of her arm backward. The man lost his grip on her and Lisa started to move back. Then, "Hey!" she said as the man's hand caught her again and clamped around her wrist. "Hey, let go of me!"

I stepped in close to the guy. "Let her go," I said. The man blinked at me, which is when Lisa seized her opportunity. She wrenched her arm free again. Then she and Voula took off. They ran to a door to the school and yanked it open. They hadn't paused long enough to say thank you, let alone to give me time to ask for a favor. Maybe I could catch up with Voula later. In the meantime, I thought, problem solved.

Then a hand closed around my upper arm and I felt myself being spun around.

"You know him," the man said.

I peered at him. He hadn't shaved in a while. His chin and jaw were covered with stubble. He hadn't combed his hair either, or changed his clothes in a day or two, judging from the look of his shirt and his pants.

"Hey, let go of me," I said. I sounded just like Lisa. I looked to Sal for support.

Sal stared at the guy. He shook his head, swallowed hard and stepped in close to me. "He's crazy," he whispered. "You can tell by his eyes."

I looked at the man again. It was true. His eyes were wild and watery, like Billy's eyes used to be when he'd had too much to drink. But there was no sour beer smell coming off this guy.

"You know him?" the man said again, only this time it came out like a question.

"Who?" I said. Sal backed off a pace and then another.

"My Robert," the man said. He pronounced it *Row-bear.*

I wanted to look at Sal, to check out where he was and what he was doing, but I didn't dare. The man's watery eyes were focused on me. He scared me a little.

"Robert?" I said. My arm was tingling. The man had a grip that could crush a boulder. "I don't know any Robert."

Wrong answer.

"You know him," the man insisted. "Everyone says they don't know him, but they do. I know they do. I know they know him. He goes to school here."

"Look, Mister—"

"My Robert," the man said. With his free hand he groped in his jacket pocket. My stomach did a flip. Now what?

The man pulled out his wallet, flipped it open and thrust it in my face. I was looking at a photo that had been tucked into a clear plastic holder in the wallet. It was a school picture. A kid with hair hanging in his eyes, a goofy grin on his face and a pimple on his chin. He was posed against the blue-gray background on the big screen they make you sit in front of while some loser photographer makes stupid cracks. Things like, *Hey, show the girls what you're made of, melt their hearts with your smile, Romeo,* saying the same thing over and over but—you have to give him credit—he tries to sound like he means it. It was the same picture they'd printed in the newspaper. Robbie Ducharme. The kid who had been kicked to death in the park.

"Mr. Ducharme?" said a voice somewhere behind me. Riel's voice. "You remember me? John Riel."

Mr. Ducharme didn't answer. He thrust his wallet at Riel.

"You know him," he said. A statement this time, not a question.

Riel stepped forward, took the wallet from the man and studied the photo. "Sure, I knew him," he said. *Knew*, not *know*. "He was a nice boy."

"He was a good boy," Mr. Ducharme said.

Riel touched Mr. Ducharme's arm, the one that was gripping me like a cop restraining a perp. Mr. Ducharme loosened his hold. Riel nodded at me. I pulled free and retreated a couple of steps.

"I'm sorry about what happened to Robbie," Riel said. He handed the wallet back to Mr. Ducharme. Mr. Ducharme ran a finger over the surface of the photograph. "He wanted to be an engineer," he said.

"He was doing so well in school." Riel said nothing.

"All he did was study," Mr. Ducharme said. "Study and play on his computer. He liked to design things, you know? He never hurt anyone. You know?"

"I know," Riel said.

"His watch was missing. Did you know that?"

Riel didn't say anything, didn't nod or shake his head.

"A watch his grandfather gave him. Whoever . . . *hurt* my Robert—" *Hurt*, like being dead was something they could cure. "They took his watch. His grandfather gave it to him for his thirteenth birthday." The man looked baffled. "You don't think they did it for the watch, do you?" he said to Riel. "You don't think that was what it was all about, do you?"

A bell rang, loud enough for everyone outside, even at the farthest edges of the yard, to hear. Riel glanced at me and nodded toward the school.

"Did you walk over here, Mr. Ducharme, or did you drive?" he said. He laid an arm on Mr. Ducharme's shoulder and steered him away from the school. When I finally went back into the building, Riel was on the sidewalk, still talking to Mr. Ducharme.

» » »

There's knowing what you're supposed to do, and then there's doing it. My Uncle Billy had always known what you were supposed to do, although that was never how he put it. What Billy always said was, "what the monkeys do." Monkey see, monkey do, Billy always said. People who worked at Walmart or Zellers or Canadian Tire— monkeys. Gas jockeys, grocery packers, auto assembly-line workers, bank tellers—monkeys, monkeys, monkeys, monkeys. Doing what they were doing because that's what they saw everyone else doing. Working at boring, soul-sucking, go-nowhere jobs day in and day out. Billy himself had been a mechanic in a garage, what some people called a grease monkey, only you didn't dare say that to Billy.

Billy was like a ghost that way—he could look in a mirror and never see himself reflected back. Doing things just because someone somewhere said you were supposed to was what monkeys did, Billy said. People—what Billy called free and independent human beings—exercised the right to choose. They did things because they *wanted* to, not because they *had* to. They answered to no one and played by their own rules, which was why Billy had gone through so many jobs. He kept getting fired for missing too many days and insisting on two rules of his own: never explain, never apologize. To be fair, though, although there were plenty of things Billy had messed up on, the bills always got paid eventually, and Billy made sure I went to school regularly and was careful to do enough things right so that the child welfare people wouldn't come around and threaten to take me away from him. But you can do all the little things right and it doesn't matter, not if you turn around and do one colossal, humongous, gargantuan thing wrong, like Billy did.

I knew what I was supposed to do. Two words—Riel's words—said it all: *Be responsible.* Meaning, Go to school. Meaning, Keep track of your stuff, get your assignments in on time, always remember that good enough really isn't good enough. Reach for the top, Mike, go the extra mile. Platitude, platitude, platitude. Meaning, Don't dump your dirty socks and underwear on the floor, put them in the hamper where they belong. Meaning, Don't just get to work on time, get there a few minutes early. Meaning, Don't just show up expecting supper to be put on the table for you, show up ready and willing and *eager* to set the table—and then clear it again afterward without being asked and stack everything in the dishwasher. And if the dishwasher is full, don't leave stuff in the sink, for heaven's sake, *unload* the dishwasher. Meaning, Don't gripe when you have to do your homework at the dining room table where I can see you, you have to *earn* privileges, Mike—and with my grades, it was going to be a real privilege to have Riel trust me to get my work done on my own in my own room with the door closed.

Riel had way more rules than my mom ever had. For sure he had more rules than Billy. And he had *standards*. Billy didn't even know what standards were. So—what choice did I have?—I had reformed. Well, mostly reformed. No one's perfect, right?

I had a job at a candy store on Danforth. Four to six, Monday through Friday; nine to one on Saturday. Minimum wage and a boss, Mr. Kiros, who freaked out if he smelled spearmint or peppermint or cherry—any candy flavor—on my breath. Mr. Kiros was a big man who ran a small printing business next door to the candy store. He was always watching the place, always worried if there were more than four or five kids in there, afraid they were going to rob him. He kept harping at me to watch the customers, make them turn out their pockets if I had to. I never did. Sure, some of the kids probably pinched candies when I wasn't looking, but I would have bet my life that most of them didn't. Besides, a guy who thought all kids were crooks, but who went ahead and opened up a place that sold cheap bulk candy, was probably in the wrong business. Double besides: Mr. Kiros's oldest son, who was seven, came into the store every day after school and stuffed his pockets with candy. Nobody ever complained about that.

Every night at six Mr. Kiros was supposed to close his printing shop and go home to his apartment above the candy store. Then Mrs. Kiros was supposed to come down and take over in the candy store. She was supposed to keep the place open until nine, while Mr. Kiros watched their three small kids. But Mrs. Kiros was almost always late coming downstairs—fifteen minutes, twenty minutes, half an hour. And this was almost always because Mr. Kiros was late closing his printing shop. He'd be out on the sidewalk, smoking a cigar and talking to a customer or a friend. I'd see him there at quarter past six and I'd know I was going to be late getting home again. It goes without saying that I never got paid for the extra fifteen or twenty minutes either, because Mr. Kiros refused to admit he was late going home, and Mrs. Kiros, who was about half the size of her husband and who seemed to be dragging herself around all the time, never contradicted him.

By the time I got home that night, it was almost quarter to seven. I smelled fried onions as I came up the walk. The smell was even stronger when I unlocked the front door and stepped into Riel's sparsely furnished but immaculate house. Riel had lived in the place for a couple of years. He hadn't done much in the way of decorating, but he sure kept the place clean. I threw my backpack down in the front hall, looked at it sitting there, then scooped it up and threw it into the hall closet. "It doesn't take any longer to put things where they belong," Riel always said.

Riel was perched on a stool at the kitchen counter. He'd made burgers—they were sitting on a broiler pan on top of the stove, ready to go into the oven. He was spinning lettuce while he watched the local news on a small TV that sat on one end of the counter.

"Sorry I'm la—" I began.

Riel held up a hand.

Okay, whatever. I grabbed a glass from the cupboard, opened the fridge and poured myself some juice.

"So far the police have no witnesses," a female voice was saying. "The investigation continues."

Riel reached for the remote and shut off the TV.

"Robbie Ducharme?" I asked. I had to bite my tongue to stop from adding, *Again?*

Riel nodded. He slid off his stool and circled the counter to the stove.

"You're late," he said.

"Mr. Kiros was late."

Riel slid the pan of hamburger patties under the broiler.

"The man wears a watch, right?" he said. I rolled my

eyes, but nodded all the same. "And he expects *you* to show up on time, right?"

"Yeah."

"Maybe you should make the point that you're expected to turn up for supper on time," Riel said. Then, before I could say anything, "Or, if he wants to adjust your hours, that's okay, but maybe he should also consider adjusting your paycheck."

"Like that's ever going to happen."

"If you don't stick up for yourself, for sure it won't," Riel said. "You want me to have a talk with him?"

"No!" I said. The last thing I needed was Riel getting involved in my work life. He was already way too involved in my school life. "I can handle it myself. Besides, he was only a few minutes late."

"Twenty, thirty minutes every day, it seems like," Riel said. "What do you think he'd do to *you* if you were twenty or thirty minutes late every day?" Then, switching gears, "Set the table, okay?"

Usually at supper Riel asked me about my day. Since he taught at my school he knew my timetable and all of my teachers. He'd ask stuff like, "Doing a unit on the law, huh? So, what do you think, the police obtain evidence without going by the book and that evidence gets thrown out even if everyone knows the guy really did it, you think that's right?"

A trick question. Testing if I'd been paying attention or if I was just swallowing everything I'd seen on TV—*American* TV. And I'd have to prove that I *had* been paying attention. Usually I'd try to get my own licks in.

"Looks like someone was asleep during law lecture at police college," I'd say. Or something like that.

Tonight, though, Riel was quiet. He worked his way through two burgers, chewing, swallowing, not smiling, not talking. Thinking, I guessed, about Mr. Ducharme and Robbie. No way was I going to start in on that topic.

» » »

Ms. Stephenson sighed.

"Act four, scene five," she said again. "Can *anyone* tell me what is going on in that scene?"

Four hands shot up. Diane Davis, Shirlene Fletcher, Bryce MacNeil, and Sam Yee. Honor roll, honor roll, honor roll, honor roll. University bound. Keeners.

Ms. Stephenson looked beyond their hands and settled on Nera Singh. I let out a great big silent sigh of relief. If she was looking at Nera, she wasn't looking at me. Sometimes that was the best you could hope for.

Nera flipped through his copy of the play, the pages *shwick-shwick-shwick*ing softly, until he found act four, scene five. I watched him squint at one page and then another while Ms. Stephenson waited. Nera's face puckered in concentration. He began to shake his head. He looked up at Ms. Stephenson, his shoulders rolled up around his ears.

"The time to read the play is *before* you come to class," Ms. Stephenson said. She turned and nodded at Sam Yee.

"Please tell us what's going on in this scene, Sam."

"Ophelia's gone crazy," Sam said. He was on the student council. Vice president of some dumb thing or other. He was one of the kids who read out school announcements over the PA system in the morning. He couldn't do it straight, either. No, he was always making lame jokes and trying to sound like whoever was the hottest comic on TV. Vin and Sal and I used to argue about who we thought he was trying to be. We almost never agreed, he was that bad.

"Ophelia's gone crazy," Ms. Stephenson repeated, in case anyone had missed Sam's brilliant answer. "Thank you, Sam." She peered around the room for her next victim. "And who would like to tell me what has driven poor Ophelia to madness?"

Many heads ducked to many books. All around me, fingers ran down lines of text in search of an answer. Jeez, I hated Shakespeare. Why couldn't we read a play in regular English, something you had at least half a chance of being able to skim?

"Mike?" Ms. Stephenson said.

I glanced down at my book, but what was the point? I wasn't going to be able to come up with the right answer. I shrugged at Ms. Stephenson and tried to look like I was sorry.

Ms. Stephenson sighed again. She also taught drama, so her breath came out like a rush of wind. She looked around again.

"Salvatore?" she said. "You look like someone who

can tell us something about the subject of madness. Would you enlighten us all, please?"

Sal had been hunched over his desk, looking like he usually did these days, like a guy who never slept, a guy who was being eaten alive by something.

"Salvatore?" Ms. Stephenson said.

Sal's head bobbed up. His eyes were red around the edges. He seemed to be making an effort to focus on her.

"Madness," Ms. Stephenson prompted. "I'm sure *you* can tell us what has driven Ophelia to madness."

Sal spasmed to a full upright position, like he'd been jolted with a stun gun. He swept the room with wild eyes. Then he jumped to his feet. He stared at Ms. Stephenson, his mouth open. For a moment it looked like he was going to say something, maybe even shout something. Then he grabbed his backpack from under his desk and bolted from the room. A couple of guys—guys in the back of the room—laughed.

"Talk about madness," someone said. More people laughed.

I stared at the door. What was with Sal? I didn't even think about it, I just stood up. Ms. Stephenson gave me a sharp look.

"Sit down," she said. She crossed to the phone on the wall beside the door. She was going to call the office. Well, let her. I grabbed my backpack and hurried after Sal.

I heard Ms. Stephenson call my name. I knew her next move would be to report Sal and me both to the office, but I didn't care. I paused in the hall for a moment and listened. I heard footsteps, faint, fading, off to the right. I headed for them and rounded the corner just in time to see a door ease shut at the far end of the hall. Sal was half a block up the street by the time I pushed my way out into the morning sun.

"Sal!" I shouted. "Hey, wait up!"

He didn't stop. He didn't even slow down. I had to really pump it to catch up with him.

"Hey, Sal!"

Sal kept pounding up the hill. He didn't glance over his shoulder, didn't give any sign at all that he had heard me. I had to grab his arm to get his attention. He shook me off like he was shaking off a bad smell.

"Hey, what's the matter with you?" I said. I was breathing hard now, trying to keep up with Sal as he motored up the hill. "Sal, hey!"

He kept ahead of me, his back to me, still pumping away so that it took a while for me to realize that his shoulders were shaking.

"Jeez, Sal—"

"Leave me alone," he said.

I picked up my pace and passed in front of him. He turned his head away, but not before I got a good look.

"You been crying?" I said. If I'd thought for half a second, I would have kept my mouth shut and saved him the embarrassment. But I was so surprised. Tear streaks were pretty much the last thing I'd expected to see on his face.

"I told you, leave me alone," he said. He spun around and shoved me, catching me off guard. He hit me hard on the chest and sent me flying backward so suddenly that I lost my balance.

My hands flew out to try to break my landing. They hit the sidewalk at the same time as my butt. My tailbone jarred against the concrete. The palms of my hands burned as they slid along the rough surface. I sat on the sidewalk, stunned at how hard he had shoved me, stunned that he had shoved me at all. I held out my hands and looked at them. The skin was scraped right off in places and grit was hammered into the wounds. It stung so bad that my eyes started to water, but there was no way *I* was going to cry, not with Sal standing right there.

He stared down at me. Then he reached out and took me by one wrist and hauled me to my feet. He didn't say anything. We walked up the hill side by side and kept going until we hit Danforth. I nodded toward the doughnut shop on the corner.

Sal shook his head. "It's on Carl's list."

Carl was the hall monitor at school. He was a retired firefighter and a nice enough guy if you weren't cutting class and he wasn't out checking all the regular places kids went when they were supposed to be sitting at a desk in math or French or history.

"No one's home at my—" I'd been going to say, at my house. But it wasn't my house. "At Riel's."

Sal nodded. He didn't say anything on the way and I didn't push him. When we got there, we didn't go inside.

Instead we circled around the house and sat on the back porch. For five minutes, maybe ten, Sal was quiet. Then he said, "The cops were at my house last night." His voice sounded funny, kind of high and trembling. "It's my dad."

Sal's dad had been in prison in Guatemala, where Sal's family is from. Sal said he had never been the same afterward. He'd been a university professor back home, but the only job he'd been able to get in Canada was office cleaner. He worked nights at a downtown office building, emptying other people's garbage, cleaning other people's toilets, dusting other people's desks. Sal said he hated it—it made him depressed.

"He's been getting worse," Sal said. He raked his nose with the sleeve of his jacket. He looked down at the floor of the porch, not at me. "He's been talking to himself a lot lately," he said. "He was like that when he got out of prison. He never talked about what happened to him in there, but he used to sit in the dark in his study, and he used to mutter to himself. He's doing it again now. My mother tries to act like everything's fine, but I can tell she's scared. My aunt keeps trying to talk him into seeing a shrink, but he won't." Sal's aunt was a doctor.

I didn't know what to say. I had met Sal's dad a couple of times. Mr. San Miguel was a small, wiry man who always seemed to be in fidgety motion. Once he had talked to me for a long time in Spanish. The only Spanish I understood was *si* and *gracias* and *una cerveca, por favor*, which I had learned from Billy after he went to

Mexico once. Later, when I asked Sal what his dad had said, Sal said it was a poem. Sal's dad had recited a poem to me in Spanish. Weird.

"Then last night, in the middle of the night, he started shouting that they were coming," Sal said.

"They?"

"I think he meant the army," Sal said. "When he was arrested that time, when he was in prison, it was the army. Soldiers came to the house to arrest him. They beat him up right there in the kitchen. My mother tried to stop them and they kicked her in the stomach. They beat him and they dragged him out of the house and we didn't see him again for three years. My mother never said so, but I'm pretty sure she thought he was dead."

I couldn't think of anything to say. I knew Sal's father had been in prison, but Sal had never gone into details. For sure he had never talked about soldiers coming to his house and beating up his father in his own kitchen. He had never talked about his mother getting kicked in the stomach either.

"He started shouting that they were coming and he grabbed the weed whacker and ran out of the house," Sal said. "This was, I don't know, two in the morning. He was out there in the yard, in his pajamas, yelling. And then the guy who lives next door came out. That guy never liked my dad. He started yelling for him to shut up, and my dad was yelling that no one was going to take him away again, no one was going to hurt his family again, but it was all in Spanish, you know, and that guy next door, he's English, he doesn't know any Spanish. So he's just yelling at my dad to shut up, it's two in the morning and normal people are trying to sleep. And he tries to grab my dad and shove him back into the house. And my dad, I don't know what he was thinking, but he goes after the guy with the weed whacker. Then the guy's wife calls the cops, and next thing you know there's cops and cop cars and people everywhere."

"Did they arrest him?" I said.

Sal shook his head. "I think they were going to. The guy next door sure wanted them to. But my mother talked to them. She convinced them not to arrest him." He kept staring at the floor. His voice dropped to a whisper. "He's pretty bad," he said. "I think he's pretty sick, you know?"

Yeah, I knew. I remembered what Sal had said about Mr. Ducharme. *He's crazy, you can see it in his eyes.* I wondered what Sal saw in his father's eyes.

"Hey, Mike?" Sal was looking at me now for the first time since we'd left school. "Don't tell anyone, okay?"

"No problem," I said.

"I mean it," Sal said. "It's bad enough, what's going on. But—"

Maybe it was because he hadn't slept much the night before. Maybe it was because he was worried. Maybe it was those things that made him look so white—Sal, whose skin is normally darker than mine, not brown exactly, but darker. It wasn't dark now, at least his face wasn't.

"You promise?"

"Yeah, I promise."

We sat on the back porch for a little longer. Then we walked over to Coxwell and had lunch at McDonald's.

"You want to go back to school?" I asked when we'd finished.

Sal shook his head. "I can get my mom to write me a note, say I was sick. What about you?" he said. "You gonna get into trouble with Riel?"

I said no, mostly so Sal wouldn't feel bad. Riel would probably hear that I had walked out in the middle of English class. He'd be mad. I'd have to tell him something. But what?

"I better go back to school," I said.

Sal didn't try to talk me out of it the way Vin would have if he and I had left school in the middle of the morning.

I was tagged by the hall monitor the minute I pushed open the door into school.

"Returning to the scene of the crime, huh, Mike?" Carl said. He shook his head, as if I were an arsonist who had come back to watch the fire I had set. Whatever.

He escorted me to the office—where I had been planning to go anyway. I knew Ms. Stephenson had reported me. I wasn't dumb enough to think I could sneak back into school and nothing was going to happen.

Mr. Gianneris gave me a detention, which he agreed to let me serve during lunch on Monday so that it wouldn't interfere with my job. Mr. Gianneris was a lot like Riel that way. To him a job was a VERY BIG

DEAL. He wasn't going to mess it up for me if he could avoid it.

» » »

For once Mrs. Kiros showed up on time to relieve me. I slung my backpack over one shoulder and headed home, cutting through a parking lot north of Danforth, then crossing the street. You could go for blocks from parking lot to parking lot in this neighborhood. As I moved from one to the other, I had to cross an alley lined on both sides with garages. As I glanced up it, I was startled to see Vin with a group of kids. I automatically raised a hand to wave, then caught myself and shoved my hand into my pocket. Vin hadn't seen me, and I wasn't sure I wanted him to. He didn't call me much anymore. Okay, so he didn't call me at all anymore. That bothered me—a *lot*. But there was nothing I could do about it. Then, just as I was wishing I was hanging with Vin and wishing at the same time that I could slip by unnoticed, he called to me.

"Mikey!"

I turned around and did my best to look surprised—*Whoa, what are you doing here?*

Vin broke away from the rest of the gang, seven or eight of them, and came smiling toward me.

"Hey, where you going?" he asked. "Come on, you want to hang out with us?"

I had to get home. Riel was expecting me. If ever I

couldn't get home on time, I was supposed to call. But I didn't have a cell phone. Riel wouldn't let me *waste*—his word, not mine—my money on one. So if I had to make a call, I'd have to find a pay phone down on Danforth.

"Hey, come on," Vin said. He threw an arm around my shoulder like he was my best pal, just like the good old days, and led me up the alley to where the rest of the gang was.

"I am not!" someone wailed. A girl. A little on the plump side. Not exactly pretty and wearing a lot of makeup to try to cover the fact. Orange hair. Tight jeans. One pierced eyebrow. Nose stud. Runny nose, swiped with the back of her hand. Downturned mouth. Smeared red lipstick.

"It's not a big deal," another girl said. Cat.

"But it's not true," the first girl said.

"If it isn't true, then why did he say it?" Cat asked. "Why would a nonentity like Bradley Tattersall tell all his loser friends in the—what is it, the *science* club?—why would he tell them that you watched a movie with him in his basement, on his couch, if it wasn't true?"

"He has a kid sister," the girl said. I couldn't remember her name. Louise? No, that wasn't right. Lu-something. Lucy. Yeah, that was it. Her name was Lucy. She was a year behind me in school. "I babysit her sometimes," Lucy said. "I was babysitting and Brad came home before his mom did, that's all."

"*Brad?*" Cat made the name sound like *honey* or *sweetheart*.

"His sister and I were downstairs watching *Muppets in Outer Space*," Lucy said. "He sat down on the couch I was on. That's all."

"Oooooh," a guy said, his voice high, imitating a girl's. The guy's name was Sly, a cool enough name until you remembered that it was short for Sylvester. Sly, another friend of A. J.'s.

Lucy's cheeks turned as red as her smeary lipstick.

"He sat on the other end of the couch from me," she said. "His mom came home, like, twenty minutes later. I left. That's *all*."

Cat's smile was wide and sympathetic.

"You've got it bad, girl," she said. "Admit it. But, hey, if you want to hang out with the Bradley Tattersalls of the world, that's your right, right?"

"And if we don't want to hang with someone who hangs with Bradley Tattersall, that's our right, too, right?" Sly said.

Cat tilted her head to one side as she thought this over.

"I guess," she said at last.

"In that case," Sly said, "I choose no." He turned to the guy next to him. A guy named Paul. "What about you?"

Paul shrugged. "Why would it matter to me who she hangs out with?" he said. But he didn't say it in a nice way, as if it was Lucy's life and Lucy's choice and everyone should leave her alone. Instead it came out like he didn't care and didn't see any reason why he should because who was she, anyway? Nobody important. Nobody who mattered. He turned and walked down the alley. Sly followed him. So did the rest of the kids, all except Cat, who hung back a little with Lucy.

"It's not true," Lucy said again. Her voice was trembling now.

"What's not true?" Cat said. "It's not true that you hung out in Bradley's basement with him? You just said you did."

"But not the way you're making it sound."

"It doesn't matter," Cat said. She flashed a smile that had nothing to do with being happy. "Nobody cares, Lucy. Nobody really cares what you do." Then she turned away, her long, thin legs carrying her over to Vin. She looped her arm through one of his, glancing at me, but barely.

"Come on," she said. "We're outta here."

Vin beamed. He stood taller now that Cat was attached to him.

"Come on, Mike," he said.

I shook my head. "I can't. I have to get home."

Cat rolled her eyes. "Come on, Vinnie," she said. *Vinnie?*

Vin slapped me on the back. "See you around," he said. He strutted away, arm in arm with Cat.

I looked back up the alley at Lucy, all alone now, sniffling, her face smeared with tears. *It's not my problem*, I told myself. I didn't even know her. Not really.

I turned to cross the street and saw a girl standing on the sidewalk, so still that it looked like she wasn't even breathing. She had a big fat beagle on a leash. Her eyes skipped from me to Vin and Cat walking up the alley, and then back to me again. She looked at me like I was something she might have to pick up with the plastic bag she had knotted to the beagle's leash.

It's not my problem, I wanted to tell her. I didn't even know this Lucy kid—and I wasn't the one who made her cry. But I didn't know this new girl, either. I told myself that I didn't care what she thought. Why should I?

CHAPTER THREE

Susan—Dr. Thomas—was in the living room when I got home. She was sliding a CD into Riel's CD player. I smiled when I saw her, and not just because I like her. Mostly I was thinking, *whew!* If she was there, Riel would be in a good mood. Riel in a good mood was a good thing. A safe thing. I realized later that I should have known better. Sure, Susan smiled right back at me. But then her eyes skipped from me to the stairs, where a moment later Riel appeared, freshly shaved and changed out of the jeans and T-shirt he had worn to school, looking more formal now in charcoal slacks and a dark shirt. He was also wearing his teacher expression—or maybe it was his cop expression—stern, verging on angry.

"You want to tell me why you cut classes today?" he said.

I glanced at Susan, who shrugged. She was always nice to me, but she never interfered when Riel was doing his foster-parent thing. She probably thought it was none of her business. I wasn't clear on her relationship with Riel. Most of the time they just seemed like good friends. But occasionally Riel would look at Susan or Susan would look at Riel and I'd think that maybe there was something more to it.

"I'm waiting for an answer," Riel said. He was at the bottom of the stairs now, arms crossed over his chest. Teacher, cop, foster-parent—he had it all nailed down with that one sharp look on his face, that one stiff way of standing.

"Sal wasn't feeling well," I said.

"Then *Sal* should have gone home."

"He did."

"Uh-huh." Riel's arms were still crossed over his chest. He was waiting for something, but I had no idea what it was.

"I walked him home," I said. "That's all. I went back to school. You can ask Mr. Gianneris."

Riel was like a bomb—solid, motionless, but you could sense the ticking, you just knew he was going to go off, and when he did . . .

"Did Sal get sick before or after you went to Mc-Donald's?"

Oh. I reran the walk to McDonald's, my mind working like a camera, panning and scanning faces on the sidewalk, faces in store windows, faces at McDonald's. I couldn't remember seeing anyone I knew. But that wasn't the right way of looking at it. The real question was, had anyone who knew Riel seen me and Sal? Riel knew a *lot* of people.

"I'm going to ask you again," Riel said. "Why did you leave school today?"

Susan slipped out of the living room and into the kitchen, leaving us alone.

I glanced at Riel and then looked down at the floor. I had promised Sal I wouldn't tell anybody about his father. Anybody meant anybody.

"Sal was having a bad day," I said at last.

"I don't want to know why Sal left school," Riel said. "I want to know why *you* left school."

"Sal's my friend."

"That doesn't answer my question."

How could I answer it? I had promised Sal. Besides, what difference did it make? I'd only missed two classes. Two. Not even a whole day.

"I'm sorry," I said.

"You bet you are," Riel said. "You're grounded for the weekend."

"Aw, come on!"

"You don't cut classes as long as you're living with me, understand, Mike?"

Yeah, I understood. I pushed by Riel and slammed up to my room. *My* room—what a joke! The room that I occupied in Riel's house.

» » »

Grounded. It sucked. Except that I wasn't totally grounded because I had my job—nine to one on Saturday—and Riel would rather grade papers for eternity than let me miss ten seconds of work. The best he could do was tell me, "You come straight home after work, do you hear me?"

It was a whole day later and Riel still sounded steamed when he talked to me, even though I had only missed two classes—and one of them was music, so it wasn't even a big deal. Mr. Gianneris had only given me a one-hour detention, which proved how minor it was. I felt like telling Riel to chill out. But Riel was the kind of guy who got more worked up when someone told him to calm down. The kind of guy who'd say, "I *am* calm," yelling the words at you, his face all red like he was going to blow an artery. So I just nodded. *Come straight home after work? Yes, sir. Whatever you say, sir.*

"And when you get home, you can clean your bathroom. And I mean really clean it this time, Mike."

Okay, so he was in *that* kind of mood. Once, when I first started living with Riel, I'd fudged a little on bathroom detail. I'd cleaned the easy stuff, the obvious stuff—a swoosh of Mr. Clean over the sink and the back of the toilet, a couple of swipes around the side of the tub. When I'd finished, the place smelled like a brigade of cleaning ladies had been through it, but I hadn't exactly hit every nook and cranny, and I hadn't attacked the grout work like my life depended on degumming it, the way Riel did. The way Riel went at everything. I'd been in a hurry. Vin had been waiting for me. Besides, how was I supposed to know that Riel would inspect the bathroom like he was a drill sergeant and I was a raw recruit?

Now he wanted me to do the bathroom the hard way?

"No problem," I said. Taking it calm, pretending it was no sweat, I could do it blindfolded and standing on one leg. "Anything else?"

"Yeah."

Of course.

"The kitchen floor. Washed *and* rinsed. And tomorrow I want you to give your room a thorough going over."

"There's just one thing," I said. "I have a project due on Monday." I'd been saving that piece of information. "I have to go to the library."

Right away I saw that Riel was conflicted. He wanted to tell me, No, you can't go, you can't go anywhere, you're grounded. But a project? Schoolwork? That was different. It was, well, it was *work*.

"What subject?"

"History."

Snap went the trap, catching Riel right where he had to care. History. The subject Riel taught. I'd been in his class right up until Riel had taken me in. I knew how seriously he took history. Vin called him Cop Boy. Mister History would have been more accurate.

"I have an essay due on World War I," I said.

"When was it assigned?"

Like that made any difference to when it was due.

"Beginning of the week," I said. "Only it's hard to get to the library when I have to work and have all my other homework. I was planning to go this weekend." A reasonable excuse followed by a reasonable plan—leaving Riel no choice but to give in.

"Okay. You can go after work. But I'm trusting you, Mike. I'm trusting you to go to the library and then to come straight home and do your chores before supper. You got it?"

Yeah, I had it.

» » »

Vin dropped by the store while I was there and bought two packages of candy cigarettes—little sticks of white sugar with a dab of red food coloring at one end that was supposed to make them look like lit cigarettes.

"You're kidding, right?" I said.

Vin grinned. "It's a joke. Cat's been bugging me. She doesn't even want to be around tobacco, let alone tobacco smoke."

"Ha, ha," I said and made change from the dollars Vin had handed me. This was, I realized, the first time in a long time that I had seen Vin alone, no A. J., no Cat, no pile of brand-new friends.

Vin pulled open one of the boxes of candy cigarettes, picking at the cardboard, trying to open it without ripping it apart so that he could close it again like a real pack of cigarettes.

"Hey, Vin?" I said.

We used to hang out together all the time. We'd been almost inseparable since kindergarten. When my mom died, Vin was cool about it. One day we were in Vin's backyard, shooting hoops at the b-ball net Vin's dad had set up at one end of the tiny yard. I don't even know exactly what triggered it. All I know is that one minute everything was cool, and the next minute I couldn't breathe because I was sobbing so hard. Vin stood for a moment on the paving stones that filled most of the yard. Stood with the basketball in his hands. Then he let go of the ball. I watched it drop to the pavement, bounce, drop back down, bounce again, *ba-dump*, *ba-dump*, *ba-dump*. Vin wrapped his arms around me— *wrapped his arms around me!*—and held onto me until I stopped crying. After that, he went inside. When he came out, he had some tissues and a couple of cans of pop. We drank them and then shot hoops until it got dark. That was Vin at eleven. Vin now—well, I wasn't so sure anymore.

Vin finally got the package of candy cigarettes open. He smiled at me as he pulled a cigarette from the box and stuck it in his mouth.

"What do you think?" he said.

"I think you look like a big baby."

"When do you get sprung from here, anyway?"

"One o'clock."

"You want to do something?" he said. "Maybe go downtown?"

"Can't," I said. "Grounded." The words came out automatically, before I realized, hey, when was the last time Vin had asked me to do something with him? And just the two of us, it sounded like.

"All *right*, Mike!" Vin said. "Still a rebel. Jeez, you had me worried there for a while, living with a cop and all." He got serious then. "He probably still knows a lot of cops, right?" he said.

"Riel? Yeah," I said. He didn't make a big point of hanging out with other cops, but I knew he knew some. "Why?"

Before he could answer, the bell above the door jangled. Three boys tumbled into the store. They looked about ten, maybe eleven years old. They fanned out through the narrow aisles, eyeing the candy, calling to each other, checking out the new stuff and the prices. The bell jangled again and two more boys came in, these two older than the first three—junior high kids, I figured. Another jangle and then there was Mr. Kiros, standing in the doorway, frowning at his customers, then frowning at me.

"You keeping an eye on things?" Mr. Kiros asked.

"Yes, sir," I said.

"Yes, *sir!*" Vin mimicked in a soft voice. Then he exploded with laughter.

"Shut up," I muttered.

"Hey, hey!" Mr. Kiros said to one of the older kids.

"You touch it, you buy it!"

The kid stared at Mr. Kiros for a moment before giving him the finger and plunging his bare hand into a bin of Reese's Pieces. Mr. Kiros charged at the kid like a rhinoceros going after a . . . well, whatever rhinoceroses go after. He wrenched the kid's arm out of the bin. Reese's Pieces sprayed out of the kid's hand, flew across the cramped store and skittered all over the floor. The kid swore at Mr. Kiros. He and his friend slammed out of the store. Mr. Kiros turned on the three younger kids, who each had a bag in their hands and had been selecting stuff from the bins—Gummi Worms and Hot Tamales and sour keys. Mr. Kiros glowered at them. The kids hung there a moment, unsure what to do.

Vin shook his head. "What a jerk," he said. "I'm outta here. Catch you later, Mikey." He was halfway out the door when Mr. Kiros grabbed him by the back of his collar.

"You," Mr. Kiros said. "Empty your pockets."

"Hey, he's okay," I said.

But Mr. Kiros didn't let go. He thrust a hand into one of Vin's jacket pockets and pulled out a package of the candy cigarettes that Vin had bought.

Vin swore at Mr. Kiros and pushed him away. Mr. Kiros must not have been expecting that because he staggered backward, thrusting out a hand to steady himself. He grabbed the edge of a bulk bin and toppled it. Sour keys spilled out all over the floor. Vin muttered something, then shoved open the door. The three smaller boys set down their bags and edged toward it too. As soon as they were close enough, they darted through it. Mr. Kiros charged the door to try to catch them. He'd decided that they were all thieves. But he lost his footing on all the sour keys on the floor and buckled to his knees. When he stood up again, slapping at his pants to get the dust and sugar off, he turned on me.

"That boy," he said, "you know him?"

"Yeah," I said. Jeez, they should have some kind of rule: if you're going to run a candy store, you should at least have to pretend that you like kids. "He's a friend of mine."

"What's his name?"

I opened my mouth to answer, but something about the question bothered me. So instead I said, "Why?"

"He stole from me."

"No he didn't."

"I told him, empty your pockets, and what does he do? Talks to me with no respect—did you *hear* what he said to me? Then he runs away." He held up the package of candy cigarettes he had taken from Vin. "What's his name?"

"He didn't steal anything," I said. "He paid for those."

Mr. Kiros's eyes narrowed. "What's his name?" he said again, only this time his voice was low, like a growl, like if I didn't tell him, he was going to bite me or something.

"No way," I said. "He didn't steal anything. He paid for that candy."

Mr. Kiros went stiff all over. His chin jutted out as he glowered at me. His face got all red. It didn't even look like he was breathing. He reminded me of a little kid holding his breath until he got his way. *He's waiting*, I realized. *Waiting for me to give up my friend for something he didn't even do. Well, forget it.* I stood behind the counter where the cash register was, looking right back at him. Vin hadn't done anything wrong. Neither had I.

Mr. Kiros must have calmed down a little because he started breathing again, big, even breaths. Maybe he wasn't as bad as I thought. It looked as if he might be willing to listen to what I was saying.

"You're fired," he said.

"What?"

"Empty your pockets," Mr. Kiros said.

"Now you think *I'm* stealing from you?" I couldn't believe it. I had been working for Mr. Kiros for nearly a month. I always showed up on time. I always stayed later than I was supposed to. And now he was accusing *me* of being a thief?

"You kids," Mr. Kiros said. "You all think you're smarter than everyone else. You think I don't check things? You think I don't know that there's a discrepancy between inventory and the cash you take in? How many of your friends come in here?"

He *was* accusing me of stealing from him—or at least of helping my friends to steal.

"It's not me," I said. "What about that kid of yours?

He comes in every day and takes a couple of dollars, worth of stuff. And what about your wife? She works here more hours than I do. Maybe she—"

Mr. Kiros could move fast for a big man. One second he was standing in front of a row of bins. The next second he was in my face, grabbing me by the arm, dragging me out from behind the counter, his hands plunging into the pockets of my jacket, then grabbing at my backpack and unzipping it and dumping everything out, spilling out my binder and pens and some homework notes. He pawed through everything while I stood there, too stunned to do anything except watch. When he didn't find anything, he shoved all of my stuff back in the backpack and thrust it at me. He didn't say he was sorry for accusing me of something I hadn't done—not that I would have accepted an apology.

I zipped up my backpack and shouldered it. My legs were shaking as I made my way to the door. I passed a display of lollipops. I imagined sweeping the whole bunch of them to the floor. My arm twitched at the thought. But I didn't do it. No way was I going to give Mr. Kiros the satisfaction of having a genuine grievance against me. I left the store without saying a word, without looking back.

I'd been planning to go to Pape Library when I finished work. It was the closest. But I was so angry about what had just happened that instead of turning south when I got to Pape, I just kept walking, crossing Carlaw and Logan, passing Chester, heading for the viaduct.

I was waiting for the light at Broadview when I saw her go by. Jen. She was sitting in the front seat of her father's BMW. Her dad was driving.

Jen.

Used to be her green eyes would sparkle at me and I would think of emeralds. Imagine that—jeez, me, a guy, and I'd look into those eyes and all of a sudden I'd be thinking of lame stuff like emeralds.

Used to be she would wrap her arms around me and lay her head against my shoulder and I'd inhale the flower-and-freshness smell of her long blond hair and feel it tickle my arms.

Used to be I'd see her down a hallway at school or across the street in the neighborhood and she'd see me and, like someone had thrown a switch, a smile would light up her face.

Used to be.

She didn't even turn her head now. I saw her framed in profile in the Beemer's front passenger-side window. Then she was gone.

The light changed. I couldn't move. Jen still had that effect on me. I'd see her and it would hit me again, hard, like a hook to the belly—she wasn't mine anymore. She had been and then, I wasn't even sure how I'd managed it, I had lost her. I knew she was gone. I knew there was no hope of getting her back. I knew it. But knowing didn't stop the ache I felt every time I saw her. It didn't keep her face from appearing in my room at night when I'd just got into bed—the worst time of the day, the time when I realized I wasn't in my own house anymore, Billy wasn't downstairs anymore, nothing was the same anymore. That's when I'd see her. And I'd think, If only . . . Then I'd think maybe there was something I could do, some way I could show her that I'd changed.

I'd been so close. I'd had a chance less than a week ago. Had it and let it slip through my fingers. I'd come out of an arcade on Yonge Street, blinking in the afternoon sun, and I'd seen a vision. At least, I'd been pretty sure at the time that it was a vision. It happened sometimes. Happened to everyone.

Once when I was twelve, I was down on Queen Street East in the Beach with Billy. Billy went into a store to get a coffee. It was a Sunday in the summer, so Queen Street was crowded with tourists and shoppers from all over. They were coming both ways on the sidewalk, wave after wave of them, heads bobbing, faces distorted by the heat that was rising in ripples from the black asphalt and the dark sidewalk. And there, right in the middle of a wave, almost knocking me off my feet with her smile, was my mother. Somewhere deep in my brain I knew it wasn't possible, she couldn't really be there. But I saw her. She was smiling at me and coming right at me. I started toward her. One of my feet actually left the sidewalk—I'd been going to rush into her arms. Then the world shifted or came into focus or the bubble popped or I woke up from my dream—whatever it was, disappointment and bitterness swelled through me, and I knew it wasn't her at all. I blinked and peered at the woman coming toward me and wondered why I had ever thought it was Mom. The woman, who was getting closer and closer and then who passed me, oblivious to me, didn't look anything like my mother.

I thought I'd seen Billy once too. I'd been walking home from school and had taken a detour up the street where Billy and I used to live. I was just coming up to the corner when I spotted him, a slight guy in jeans and a T-shirt, shaggy blond hair hanging in his eyes. My heart had started to hammer in my chest. Billy. It was Billy!

Except it wasn't.

It was just some guy I'd never seen before. A guy with brown eyes instead of blue eyes, with a narrow face instead of Billy's rectangular face, with a hookish nose instead of Billy's bent and crushed nose.

So when I came out of the arcade on Yonge Street almost a week ago and blinked in the sun and thought I saw Jen, looking down the street, not noticing me, I thought I was seeing things again.

Then she turned—pirouetted—and in that movement, fluid from all those years of ballet lessons she had taken, I knew I wasn't seeing things. It was really her. She pirouetted, pushed off, and then all I saw was her long blond hair swaying in sync with her hips.

I could have called her name: "Hey, Jen!"

Before, if I'd done that she would have flashed me a smile, would even have thrown herself into my arms if her mood was right and I hadn't done anything stupid lately. But now? Now I wasn't sure how she'd react. What if she was on her way to meet some of her rich drive-their-own-cars private school friends?

But what if she wasn't? What if she was just heading to HMV or the Eaton Centre or any one of a hundred stores? What if she was on her way to the subway? What if she was about to go home? If she was, and if I let her get away one more time, I'd never have a chance to talk to her. Her mother was like a jailer or a gatekeeper—or a Rottweiler or a pit bull. To get at her, you had to go through Mrs. Hayes. Jen had a cell phone, but she must have changed the number because when I tried it, I always got a message that said No Service. I'd screwed up enough courage to ask Jen's friend, Voula, but she wouldn't tell me anything. Her answer, delivered in that snotty tone some girls have nailed down: "If she'd wanted you to have the number, she would have given it to you."

But now there she was, Jen, for the first time in over a month. All alone, no girlfriends around. No boyfriends, either.

I went after her.

Down Yonge Street. Across Dundas. Into the Eaton Centre. It was easier to track her in there. The place was crowded with shoppers, and I could always turn away and pretend to be studying a jacket in the window of Gap or Old Navy if she started to turn.

She walked straight through the north mall, down the main mall, through the food court, out the other end, and down the short escalator into the subway station. Then she surprised me. She stopped, boom, like she'd run into a wall. She looked right, then left. Then she ducked into a pay phone. Why a pay phone when she had her own cell phone?

There were two phones set almost back-to-back into slots in the wall. Jen was in one of them, her back to the opening. I ducked into the other. I lifted the receiver and pretended to be using it when, really, I was eavesdropping.

I missed the beginning of her phone call and had to strain to catch what she was saying.

Midnight. I definitely heard her say midnight. She sounded surprised, even a little nervous. Midnight, sure, she could do that. I strained to hear every sweet word she said, to hear her voice that lilted musically even though I could tell she was nervous, maybe even upset, about something. Then, faintly, a *thunk*, followed by silence.

I froze. I kept the phone pressed to my ear and my back turned to the opening in case she doubled back the way she had come. Seconds slipped by. When I had counted out enough of them to make a minute, I turned. There was no sign of Jen. I dropped the receiver into its cradle and stepped out of the slot. She was gone.

She was always gone.

As I walked across the viaduct now, I had a picture of her in my mind—Jen, framed in profile in the front passenger-side window of her dad's BMW. Jen staring straight ahead, not smiling.

Jen with something serious on her mind.

Just like me.

CHAPTER FOUR

"What goes on in your head, Mike?" Riel said. He was at the door when I pushed it open and he started in on me right away with his questions: *Do you have any idea what time it is? Did you forget that you're supposed to be grounded? You were supposed to go to work, go to the library, then come right home and do your chores—does that ring a bell, Mike?* And now this: "What goes on in your head, Mike?"

The same stuff as goes on in anyone else's head—jeez, what did he think? Why did adults even bother asking questions like that? Probably because they always came off looking superior. Because questions like that were impossible to answer. Questions like that left kids with nothing to do but shrug and look stupid.

"Did you think you could just breeze in here any old time and there'd be no consequences?" Riel said. He was angry. I could see that by the pinched look around his eyes and by how tight his lips were, even when he was shooting off question after question. But he wasn't yelling. With Riel, the angrier he got, the quieter he talked.

"I got fired," I said.

His eyes widened a little. He hadn't been expecting that, and it was always nice to see Riel—a smart guy who knew he was a smart guy—get caught off guard and have to rethink things a little. Which was part of the reason I said it. I also said it because maybe Riel would think getting fired was the reason I'd been gone so long and because maybe if he calmed down enough to hear the whole story, he'd cut me a little slack. I said it, too, because I still couldn't believe it. And I said it so I'd have something else to think about besides that picture of Jen, framed in the window of her dad's Beemer. Something besides that whole thing with Jen.

"Fired?" Riel said. His lips weren't so tight anymore either. "What happened?"

What happened? Not, *What did you do?* Or, *How did you manage to screw up again?* Just when you thought you had him figured out—Mr. Rigid, Mr. Model Foster Parent, Mr. Strict Disciplinarian—Riel could still hand you a surprise.

I told him the whole story. He flinched when I mentioned Vin's name. Riel didn't have the highest opinion of Vin, mainly because the biggest trouble I ever got in, I'd got in because of Vin. But he didn't say anything. He didn't interrupt while I explained that Vin hadn't done anything, that, as far as I could tell, none of the kids had done anything until after Mr. Kiros started in on them.

"So, basically," Riel said when I finished, "he fired you because he was mad at some other kids, because Vin is your friend, and because he thought you were stealing from him?"

"Yeah," I said. "Basically."

Riel nodded. He chewed over the information some more. "Well," he said, "it sounds to me as if he was totally unjustified in what he did. If you want to, you can try to fight him on it. Try to get your job back."

Having a job was important to Riel. So was standing up for yourself. I knew that. But Mr. Kiros was pretty hard to take at the best of times. Forcing him to give me back my job wasn't going to improve the situation.

"Maybe I should just get another job," I said.

"You sure?"

"Yeah, I'm sure. My resume is still on the computer. I can hand it out tomorrow after school." I hesitated. "I guess I won't be able to use Mr. Kiros's name, though." I'd been hoping for a good reference from the candy store job—if there was one thing I needed, it was a good reference. But it didn't look like that was going to happen.

"Guess not," Riel said. "Sorry it turned out that way, Mike." He glanced at his watch. "You still have time to clean your bathroom before supper," he said. "You can do the kitchen floor tomorrow."

Right, I thought. *Along with all the other stuff.*

» » »

"Looks like the cops caught a break," Riel said Monday morning. He was sitting at the kitchen table, freshly showered, his hair still damp, drinking coffee. He smiled up at me like he hadn't turned me into Cinderella for the weekend—*scrub the floor, clean out the garage, bag the garbage*—like maybe we were even best friends.

"What do you mean?" I said. I was at the fridge, trying to decide between no-sugar-added orange juice and organic milk.

"The Robbie Ducharme case," Riel said.

I finally chose the orange juice. I reached for a glass from the cupboard.

"You mean, they know who did it?"

Riel shook his head. "Doesn't say. But someone—a girl, apparently—went by the park that night. She saw kids coming out of the park."

Somehow I lost my grip on the juice jug. It hit the floor and bounced up again, slopping orange juice everywhere. Riel looked at it, then at me, and started to get up.

"It's okay," I said. "I'll get it." After all, it wasn't like I didn't know where the mop was. Besides, I needed the distraction. While I mopped, I said, "Kids? You mean this girl doesn't know them?"

"Paper doesn't say. It just says she saw kids."

"Doesn't sound like much of a break," I said.

"It's progress. It's been nearly a week, and all that time, no one saw anything. Now we have someone who definitely saw kids."

We? Riel had quit being a cop a few years ago, but he still got all wound up when there were articles in the paper about cops or about major cases. Sometimes, if you ask me, it seemed that maybe Riel regretted his decision. But if he did, he sure wasn't sharing that information with me.

"You should have something to eat," Riel said. "Have some cereal."

By cereal, Riel didn't mean Cocoa Puffs or Count Chocula. He meant health-food-store granola. Served with yogurt. Nonfat yogurt.

"No thanks," I said. "I'm not hungry." Which was true, for a whole lot of reasons.

» » »

I found Sal at my locker at lunchtime, spinning the dial of my combination lock, yanking on the lock, looking confused when the lock didn't give.

"Hey," I said. "I reformed, remember?"

In the good old days, the pre-Riel days, half the school had my locker combination. I didn't care. Heck, I *gave* it out. If people went in my locker, books went missing. Notes went missing. Assignments went missing. People took stuff. Took my stuff. Which made me a victim, right? And you never, ever blame the victim, right? In the pre-Riel days, I didn't care much about school. Billy didn't care either. Sure, he pushed me to show up. But that was because "If you don't show, I get blamed, Mikey. That makes me look like I can't take care of you. And the minute they think that, I'm history. They'll take you away. You don't want to end up in foster care, do you, Mikey?"

No, I never wanted that. That hadn't stopped it from happening, though.

"It doesn't matter," Sal said, releasing his hold on my lock. "I wasn't looking for anything." He spun the dial a few more times. "Except maybe can I have my English notes back?"

"Yeah," I said. "Sure." I took the lock into my hand and was surprised when Sal turned his back so that I could dial my combination in private. Jeez, Sal was a good guy. Responsible. If Riel really got to know Sal, he'd love him. "You don't have to do that," I said.

"I don't want to be tempted."

"Yeah, but I trust you." And I did. It was true. I trusted Sal 100 percent. Which was funny when I thought about it. If you asked me who's your best friend, it was a no-brainer. I'd say Vin. Vin and I went all the way back to kindergarten. Only now, the way things were turning out, I wasn't so sure. But when I had changed locks, Vin had pestered me for the combination, *in case of emergency*, he said. And the next thing I knew, I was in class without a history book. Sal, though? Sal didn't even ask for the combination. I looked at his back, yanked on the lock until it gave, and thought, *Maybe Sal is my best friend now. Maybe things have shifted that much.*

"So, did you bring it?" Sal said as he turned around.

Jeez. "No, I forgot."

"But you said you'd bring it." Sal was looking better now. He seemed a little more back to normal, and not just because his eyes weren't all watery and bloodshot. He seemed back to normal because he was giving me a hard time for not bringing the money to buy a ticket to the school dance.

"I forgot. I'll bring it tomorrow," I said.

"What if they sell out?"

There was a limit to how many kids could attend school dances. You had to buy a ticket, and when the tickets were all gone, you were out of luck.

"It's *Monday*," I said. The dance wasn't until Friday.

"Tickets sold out on Monday for the last dance," Sal said. The last dance had had an actual band instead of recorded music. I figured maybe that was why it had sold out so fast.

"It'll be fine," I said. "I'll bring it tomorrow for sure."

"Now," Sal said. "You gotta get the money now."

"But I don't have it." Jeez, hadn't I just said that? For some reason that I didn't understand, Sal was desperate to go to this dance. He was just as desperate to drag me along with him. It had to be a girl. A girl he had it bad for but hadn't told me about yet. I tried to think of who it could be, but drew a blank.

"Fine," I said. "This is such a big deal to you, *you* lend me ten bucks?"

"I don't have that much money," he said.

So what was I supposed to do? If I could figure out how to pluck ten dollars out of thin air whenever I needed it, well, life would be a whole lot different, right?

"Ask Riel," Sal said.

I shook my head. Riel was funny about money—especially about me asking for money when that was the whole point of me having a job. But it wasn't like I'd be asking him to *give* me money. It was only a loan, ten bucks. I could pay him back when I got home. And the money wasn't for anything Riel would disapprove of. It was for a school dance. School dances contribute to school spirit. School spirit is a good thing. Riel is as big on school spirit as he is on school sports.

"Okay," I said.

"Ask him *now*."

"O-kay," I said.

I tried the staff lounge first. I knocked on the door and asked politely when—who else?—Ms. Stephenson answered. It just had to be Ms. Stephenson. It couldn't have been Mr. Korchak, my music teacher, who actually seemed to like me. Ms. Stephenson seemed only too happy to tell me that Riel wasn't there.

I tried Riel's classroom, but he wasn't there either, and the room was locked. I could have quit then. I'd tried, right? But Sal was going to pop an artery if I didn't produce ten bucks and buy a dance ticket by the end of the day.

Maybe Riel was outside. Riel was also very big on outside.

But, no, he wasn't there either.

Now I was really baffled. He had to be somewhere. One thing about Riel, he was 100 percent responsible. When he was supposed to be at school, he was at school. But where at school?

I tried the gym. Then the office. I peeked through the window in the door to the auditorium. I didn't see Riel, but I was willing to bet serious money that the briefcase that was sitting on the stage was his. Curious—where there's briefcase, there's teacher—I pushed open the door. The auditorium seemed deserted. I stood at the back for a moment, quiet, listening, and finally caught the hum of a voice. A masculine voice, coming from up near the stage. Riel? If so, what was he up to?

I crept up the aisle—which was easy in sneakers—until Riel's voice became clearer.

"It was the right thing," he was saying.

What was the right thing? Who was he talking to?

"But it was in the paper," another voice said. A woman, maybe. Maybe a girl. Her voice quavered. "It took me four whole days to tell my mother. Then my mom and dad argued about it, you know?"

Argued about what? Who was Riel talking to? And why were they talking in here, of all places? Why not out in the open? Why not in Riel's classroom?

"My mom, she wanted me to call the police right away. My dad was dead against it. He said, what good would it do, especially if I didn't see anyone clearly enough to identify them? He said, what if one of them saw me clearly, though? He really scared me, Mr. Riel. I mean, what if he's right? What if those kids I saw were the ones who killed that boy? And what if they saw me? I mean, it says in the paper the police have a witness who saw kids in the park. What if one of them recognizes me and thinks I know something?"

So, *she* was the one.

Riel didn't jump right in with an answer, which didn't surprise me. Sometimes when you asked Riel a question—a serious question, not a have-you-seen-my-math-book question—he would just look at you, like he was the one who had asked the question and now he was waiting for you to answer it.

"But I couldn't just say nothing, could I?" the girl said. I was sure it was a girl now. A student at this school. Maybe even someone I knew. "I mean, my mom's right, right? You have a duty to come forward, right?"

Another few heartbeats of silence. Then, "You did the right thing, Rebecca."

I ran through every girl I knew. There were no Rebeccas.

More silence. Then, "It's just that . . ." Silence. "They *killed* a kid, Mr. Riel." More silence. A whole long stretch of it. And this time it was Riel who broke it.

"It's not always easy doing the right thing," he said. "If you're worried about anything, if you feel something isn't right, if you get scared, you can call the police. The detective you talked to gave you his card, didn't he? If anything comes up, you call him. Or come and see me.

And next time, I think it would be okay if you saw me in my classroom."

I heard a scraping sound. Chairs, maybe. Maybe they had been sitting down and now they were getting up. I started to back away from the stage.

The girl appeared just like that—now you see her, now you don't. She stepped out onto the stage. Maybe she'd been planning to jump down off it, but she froze when she saw me. I recognized her immediately. She was the girl I had seen in the alley the day that I'd run into Vin. The girl with the fat beagle. She wasn't giving me the same look as she had that day, though, like I was something nasty to be scooped up off the street. Instead, she looked scared. She had a long, slender neck—I don't know why I noticed that, but I did—and her head turned on it as she glanced back at Riel, who was coming out onto the stage to retrieve his briefcase. Riel frowned when he caught the expression on her face. "Mike, what are you doing here?" he said. Then he nodded at the girl, a little gesture that said, it's okay, nothing to worry about, off you go.

Rebecca—I wondered what her last name was—jumped down off the stage and landed without a sound. She hurried up the aisle to the door without looking at me. When she got to the door, she stopped and peeked out, head moving right, then left. Only then did she push her way out into the hall.

"Is she the one?" I said. I tried to sound casual, like it was no big deal, so that there'd be more of a chance that

Riel would answer.

Riel made a lot more noise than Rebecca when he jumped down from the stage—*ba-bump*.

"Were you eavesdropping?" he said.

I shook my head. Deny, deny, deny. "I was looking for you, that's all," I said. "I need to borrow ten dollars for a dance ticket."

Riel's gray eyes drilled into me.

"Okay," I said. What was the point? It was obvious he knew. "Okay, so I heard some of what she said. But I wasn't eavesdropping. I mean, I didn't come in here to spy on you or anything."

"That's good," Riel said. "Because anything Rebecca said to me was said in confidence. And I would hate to have that confidence betrayed. It would reflect badly on me. You hear me, Mike?"

"Yeah, I hear you." Then, I couldn't help myself: "She didn't recognize anybody?"

"I said she spoke to me in confidence," Riel said. It was all he said. Well, fine. Time to change the subject.

"So," I said, "can you lend me ten dollars for a dance ticket? I'll pay you back when I get home."

Riel dug his wallet out of his pocket and pulled out a couple of fives. "You didn't see Rebecca here and you didn't see her talking to me, right?"

"Sure," I said. Whatever.

» » »

I was standing outside the west entrance of the school when Rebecca Whatever-her-last-name-was came through the door at three thirty. I hadn't been looking for her. I had just come outside, the way any normal kid does when the final bell of the day rings. I had seen Vin standing there, probably waiting for Cat, and I had stopped to tell him about what had happened at the candy store, about getting fired. Vin thought that was pretty funny. He was laughing when Rebecca came out the door.

It was pure coincidence that I happened to be there. If I hadn't spotted Vin, I would have kept walking. I would have been halfway home by the time that door opened. But the way Rebecca's eyes widened, the way they bugged right out of her head and the wild way she scanned the schoolyard behind me looking for—what? friends? protection? witnesses?—told me that she didn't think it was an accident that I was there. I backed up a few paces, to put distance between myself and her, and felt like throwing up my hands, surrendering, to show I meant no harm.

"Hi, how's it going?" I said, trying to sound friendly. What was with her, anyway? Why was she treating me like I was the entrance to a dark alley in a lonely part of town at two in the morning?

Her legs beat triple-time, like windshield wipers in a major downpour, as she blew past me.

"What's with her?" Vin said.

She was scared, that's what was with her. She had

looked at me like she was staring down the barrel of a loaded gun. I wanted to run after her and tell her to calm down, tell her I wasn't going to do anything to her, relax.

"Yeah," said a voice behind me. A girl's voice this time. "What's up with her?"

It was Cat. I didn't know how long she had been standing in the doorway. She smiled at me. At least, I thought it was a smile.

CHAPTER FIVE

The next day after school, I went into every store on Gerrard Street and on Danforth where I thought I might have a shot at a job—candy stores, video stores, doughnut shops, the McDonald's down near Coxwell, even the Italian supermarkets—to drop off a resume and maybe talk to someone, an owner or a manager. I wasn't exactly greeted with lots of enthusiasm. But then, I hadn't expected much. When I ran out of resumes, I headed home.

The first thing I saw when I came through the door and glanced into the living room, halfway to dropping my backpack on the floor before remembering that Riel would chew me out until I picked it up again and put it where it belonged, was a pair of boots. Boots belonging to someone who was sitting in an armchair angled away from the door. Boots on feet at the ends of legs wearing a business suit. Not Riel's boots. Riel had company.

"Mike, is that you?" he called from the living room.

"Yeah."

"Come in here a minute."

I stepped into the doorway. Riel was sitting on the couch. Opposite him, in a high leather armchair, was a man I had met back before I moved in with Riel. He was a cop. A homicide detective Riel called Jonesy.

"Mike, you remember Detective Jones?"

Yeah, I remembered him.

"He wants to talk to you." Riel's eyes were fixed hard on me. What was that about?

Detective Jones swung up out of his chair. He was taller than Riel, bulkier, a large and ominous presence. But he was smiling.

"Come on in, Mike," he said. "Have a seat."

Why was he being so friendly when Riel was looking so—what? Worried? Was that what it was? I sat down on the couch next to Riel.

"John tells me you're doing better in school," Detective Jones said.

I glanced at Riel. "Yeah, I guess," I said.

"That's good," he said. "I hear you got a new history teacher too."

Uh-huh. Was I really supposed to believe that Riel had called me in to give Detective Jones a rundown on my life at school? What next? Was he going to ask for my opinion on Mr. Danos, my new history teacher? Mr. Danos was due to retire next year. Not a minute too soon, if you ask me. The guy wasn't anywhere near as enthusiastic about history as Riel was. I used to think that Riel was *too* enthusiastic for a subject that wasn't just as dry as dust, it *was* dust. I didn't realize, until I was transferred into Mr. Danos's class, that too little enthusiasm is definitely worse than too much.

"Detective Jones is investigating Robbie Ducharme's death," Riel said.

A-ha. I looked at the detective with new interest. Detective Jones was on the job. Okay. But what was he doing here? Comparing notes with an old colleague?

"He wants to ask you some questions, Mike."

"*Me?*"

Then, before I knew it, Detective Jones was telling me, since I was a juvenile, that he had to caution me. Did I understand what that meant? He said it was standard procedure. He told me that I had the right to have Riel present, as my guardian, while I answered his questions, and that I had the right to counsel too, if I wanted it. He asked me, Did I understand that, did I know what right to counsel was? He didn't accept a nod of my head either. He made me explain it to him.

Just to be perfectly clear, I asked, "Am I in trouble?" A stupid question, I knew. Stupid because even a first-grader could figure out that when a homicide detective is cautioning you, that should be your first clue that all is not well in your own little corner of the universe.

"That depends," Detective Jones said. He wasn't smiling anymore. "You want to tell me where you were last Tuesday night, Mike?"

What? Why was he asking that? What was going on?

"I was here," I said, glancing at Riel.

"All night?"

That's what I had told Riel when he'd asked me the day after Robbie Ducharme had been kicked to death. I wanted to look at him, but I didn't. Instead I looked right at Detective Jones and said, "All night."

"You sure, Mike?" Detective Jones had pale blue eyes. They were focused 100 percent on me. They didn't waver even for a second.

Was he asking me about Robbie Ducharme? Was that what was going on? So what if it was? No one had seen anything. And since no one had seen anything, there was no point in making myself look worse than I usually looked.

"Yeah," I said. Was it my imagination or did my voice sound higher than normal? "Yeah, I'm sure."

"Because, you know, Mike, we've been pulling out all the stops on this Robbie Ducharme thing. You knew Robbie, didn't you?"

"Not really," I said. "He was in my math class. I never hung around with him or anything. I don't think you could say I knew him, not the way I know my friends." Which was true.

"Lots of people knew Robbie and didn't know him," Detective Jones said. "Funny, huh?"

I didn't say anything. I didn't understand what he was getting at.

"We put out an appeal to the public," Detective

Jones said. "You've heard of Crime Stoppers, right?"

Who hadn't?

"We got a lot of calls," Detective Jones said. "One of them was a man who'd been out of town for a couple of days. When he got back, he was watching TV. He saw the Crime Stoppers segment on Robbie Ducharme and he called the number. He said he'd been on his way home that night from a friend's house and was walking by the park. He said he saw a kid on the street near the park late at night. The same park where Robbie Ducharme was killed."

I had to fight to keep from squirming under the steady gaze of Detective Jones's pale blue eyes. Where was this going?

"He gave us a pretty good description," Detective Jones said. He peered hard at me now. "We had him go through the yearbooks of some of the schools in the area, to see if he recognized the kid."

Jeez, I whispered to myself, don't let this be going where I think it's going.

"And, what do you know," Detective Jones said. "He picked out someone." The pause that followed was so long that it qualified as torture. "He picked out your picture, Mike. Says he's positive you were the kid he saw."

I didn't dare look at Riel. I didn't dare look at Detective Jones either, except that I had the feeling that if I didn't, he'd think I was guilty of something. So I made myself meet his eyes. I made myself look surprised. I made myself—*tried* to make myself—look like I had done nothing wrong.

"You want to tell me how come, when you say you were here, we have a guy who swears he saw you walking near the park?" Detective Jones said.

Relax, Mike, I told myself. *This isn't as bad as it seems. True, this is where I have to admit that I lied to Riel. But that's okay. I can handle that. There's a big difference between being caught in a lie and being a serious suspect in a killing.*

"Tuesday?" I said.

"Yeah," Detective Jones said. He sounded like he recognized my question for what it was—a stalling tactic. "I'd like you to account for your actions on Tuesday, from the time you left school."

I sneaked a look at Riel, whose face betrayed no emotion. "Well, I went to work," I said. "At the candy store, you know?"

Detective Jones shook his head. He didn't know. I told him the name of the store and Mr. Kiros's name too, in case he wanted to check. Detective Jones wrote down what I said.

"Then I came home," I said. I had taken the long way home, the way that led through Jen's neighborhood and along her street. Call me a loser, but I had been hoping to catch a glimpse of her. I knew it was crazy. I knew she didn't want anything to do with me. But I couldn't shake her loose from my mind. From my heart. So I walked down her street and I spotted her with her friend Ashley. They were walking together up the path to Ashley's house. Ashley was carrying some rolled-up pieces of poster board. Jen was wearing her backpack and carrying the little suitcase that she used when she was sleeping over at a friend's house. But I didn't tell Detective Jones that. I didn't want Riel to know I was so pathetic that I still had a thing for Jen. Besides, it didn't have anything to do with Robbie Ducharme.

"Then I had supper and cleaned up and did my homework. Then I went to my room," I said.

Detective Jones waited. I felt Riel's eyes on me too, like lasers, probing me.

"Then, I don't know, I couldn't sleep," I said and gave a little shrug. The idea I was trying to convey was: it's no big deal, stuff like this happens every day of the week to all kinds of people. I focused on Detective Jones and tried not to think about the expression on Riel's face. "So I decided to take a walk."

Riel shifted on the couch beside me, but he didn't say anything.

"You couldn't sleep?" Detective Jones said. "You want to tell me about that?"

I shrugged again. I had never worked so hard at trying to seem casual. "It happens sometimes. You know, since Billy . . ." I let my voice trail off. Detective Jones knew all about what had happened to Billy. He had been involved. "Sometimes when it happens, when I start thinking about Billy, I just turn on the TV," I said. "But, I don't know, Tuesday night I just had to get out of here." I wondered what Riel would think of that, whether he'd be hurt or offended. "So I got dressed and I—" I dared a half-glance at Riel, looking in his direction but not looking directly at him, not wanting to confirm what I thought he might be thinking. "I left the house," I said. I tried to imagine the expression on Riel's face—was he shocked, was he disappointed, or was this pretty much what he had figured? Not that it mattered. The bottom line was: I had lied to him. Now, because he knew I had lied, I murmured, "Sorry."

"What are you sorry for, Mike?" Detective Jones said.

I didn't answer right away. Riel knew. That was enough.

"Mike?" Detective Jones said again.

"I got dressed," I said again. That much was true. "I left the house." Also true. "And I took a walk."

"Where did you walk?"

"Over to my house." *My house.* Like I had ever owned the place. Like I still did. But I didn't. I never had. Neither had Billy. It had just been the place where we lived.

Detective Jones glanced at Riel. Riel didn't say anything.

"Go on, Mike," the detective said.

I looked down at the white and black rug on Riel's living room floor.

"I just stood there for a while, looking at the place." It was something I had done a million times since I'd moved in with Riel. "I just stood there, you know?" Stood there and remembered. My mother, the smell of supper cooking, Billy, the screen door with the ripped screen, the fridge that always held a dozen past-best-date jars of pickles and mustard and relish and sauerkraut—Billy loved to pile mustard and sauerkraut on his hot dogs—but that never seemed to hold any real food. Nothing you'd recognize from the Canada Food Guide that they made you memorize at school.

"How long were you there, Mike?"

"I don't know." Forever. Never. Some time in between.

"Then what did you do?"

Okay, now I could look Detective Jones in the eyes because now I had nothing to worry about.

"Then I walked around," I said. "I—I guess I might have walked down past the park. It's half a block from my house." There, I had said it again. *My house.*

"So you *were* at the park that night?"

"Yeah." Better to admit it, right? "Yeah, I guess I walked by it."

"Did you see anyone else at the park?"

I shook my head.

Detective Jones was leaning back in his chair, legs crossed, looking relaxed. Far more relaxed than Riel. He had a notebook on his lap and a pen in his hand, but he had only made a few notes. He didn't say anything now. He seemed to be waiting for me to speak. What did he want me to say? I held my tongue while he twirled his pen.

Finally he said, "What time did you leave here, Mike?"

"I dunno." Not true. I knew exactly. I knew to the minute. "Maybe eleven." I said eleven because Riel had told me he'd heard me—he'd either heard me leave or heard me return. Either way, he'd heard me and he had probably already told Jonesy, so there was no point in lying about when I had left and when I'd got back.

Detective Jones made a note in his notebook.

"So at eleven o'clock on Tuesday night, you left the house, is that right?" he said.

I nodded.

"And you went straight to your old house?"

"Yeah."

"You remember the route you took, Mike?"

I nodded again. I remembered every detail of Tuesday night.

"You want to tell me?"

I described a route that would take me more or less directly from Riel's house to the house where I had lived with Billy and, before that, with my mother.

Detective Jones made more notes.

"And what did you do when you got there?"

I glanced at Riel. I'd already answered that question. Why did I have to answer it again? Riel nodded brusquely. The message: just do it.

"I just stood outside. I—" Make it sound good. "I was just thinking about Billy, that's all."

"Anyone see you?"

I shook my head.

"Then, from there, where exactly did you go?"

Jeez, so many questions. Questions that I had already answered.

"I walked around," I said.

"Do you remember where you walked?"

I looked down at my knees. Where did I walk? Okay . . .

"Around," I said. "Over to Greenwood, down to Queen, then along Queen—"

"Heading east or west?"

"East," I said. Why not?

"Then, I dunno, up Coxwell, along the park, home."

"And you got home at what time?"

"Two," I said. "I got home around two."

Detective Jones wrote down all of that.

"Did you go into the park?"

"No. I just walked by it."

"You didn't go into the park?"

"No."

"Did you see anyone in the park when you walked by?"

"No."

"No one at all?"

"No one."

Detective Jones looked me over, looked at my face closely, probably trying to decide if he believed me. Looked at my hands too, which I was holding on my lap. For a minute I thought he was going to ask me about them. But apart from a scab on one knuckle, they were pretty much back to normal. He leaned back in his chair. The hand holding the pen relaxed. "Is there anything else you want to tell me, Mike?"

"Like what?"

"Anything at all. Anything you think might be important."

I shook my head. There was nothing. "Can I go now?" I said.

"Sure," Detective Jones said.

I stood up. Detective Jones stayed in his chair. He was going to talk to Riel, I realized. The two of them were probably going to talk about me. I headed for the kitchen. Maybe from there I'd be able to hear what they said. But before I got halfway there, Riel said, "Go up to your room, Mike. Get a start on your homework."

It was an order, I knew, not a suggestion.

» » »

When Riel came upstairs after seeing Detective Jones out, he did pretty much what I expected him to do. He stood in the door to my room, his hands hanging at his sides, peering at me with a big frown on his face, like he'd just discovered that a stranger was living in his back bedroom and he was wondering where he'd come from and what the best way was to deal with the situation. He looked pretty much the way I expected he'd look too—angry, suspicious, disappointed. The anger didn't bother me much. People who got angry didn't usually stay angry. Eventually they calmed down. It took some people longer than others to shake off their anger, but they always did. Always.

Suspicion and disappointment, though, those were

different. When people caught you in one lie, they couldn't help it, they started wondering how many other lies you had told them, how often you had betrayed their trust, how big or how little those lies were and what it said about them that they had believed you. And disappointment—well, disappointment is worse than anger, because when a person is disappointed in you, it's because they expected better. They actually had confidence in you. They were in your corner. They knew you were a good person. So when it turned out that you weren't so good after all, that you hadn't lived up to their expectations, the disappointment they felt was really disappointment on your behalf. Their disappointment meant that *you* had failed.

I glanced at Riel when he first appeared in the doorway. Then I ducked back down to my math textbook. Go and do your homework, Riel had said. So, okay, I had come up here and I had taken out my homework books. But I couldn't make myself concentrate. Not when I knew what was coming. And now that it was here, I couldn't make myself face it. I just couldn't look at Riel.

Seconds ticked by and still Riel was silent. I knew exactly what was going on. He was waiting for me to say something. Probably to apologize. Definitely to explain.

"I'm sorry," I said without looking at him. I don't think I had ever been sorrier.

Nothing. Riel was still there. I could sense his presence. But I couldn't read the expression on his face unless

I looked at him and, I couldn't believe it, but I was scared to do that. I was scared to look at Riel again. Scared to see that suspicion and that disappointment again. But I had to, didn't I? I couldn't sit there like a coward, like a baby, with my head down, pretending I was doing math—like anyone was going to believe that!—when really what I was doing was wishing Riel would tell me, *Hey, it's no problem, stuff happens, right?* So I forced myself to look up. It was the hardest thing I had done in a long time. And then, maybe because of that wounded look on Riel's face, I got mad myself.

"It's not your fault, if that's what you're worried about," I said.

"Excuse me?" Riel said. He couldn't have sounded more surprised if I'd just produced a birthday cake, complete with lit candles, and started singing.

"Anything I do, it's not your fault," I said. "In case you're worried that your friends will think it is." I was thinking about Detective Jones. He and Riel knew each other back from when Riel was still a cop.

Riel seemed to consider this carefully. He considered it for so long that I knew it had been a mistake to say it.

"Actually," he said, with a kind of scary calm, "worry isn't exactly the emotion that I'm experiencing right now." His eyes locked onto mine. "In fact," he said, talking slowly, slowly, like the words rattling around in his mind were a pack of wild dogs and he had to keep a firm leash on them, otherwise they'd rip me to pieces, "I'm a little more concerned about you than I am about me."

The shame that I felt was like sharp-toothed little animals gnawing at my insides.

"Have I ever been other than completely honest with you, Mike?" Riel said.

I thought about all the time I had known Riel. He always told the truth, even when it was unpleasant or it hurt. Maybe when it came to riding me about my schoolwork or my job or keeping my room clean, he treated me like a kid who needed a firm hand. But in everything else, he treated me like an intelligent human being—he never talked down to me, never took the attitude that I couldn't possibly understand, and he never, ever lied to me.

I shook my head.

"So how come you lied to me about the other night?" Riel said. "How come you didn't just tell me how you were feeling? How come you didn't tell me that you'd gone out?"

The best I could do was offer a slow, rolling, ashamed shrug and a lame, "I thought you'd be mad."

"Anything else you want to tell me, Mike?"

I had to look directly at him now. I had to if I wanted to win back his trust.

"No," I said.

"You sure?"

"I didn't have anything to do with what happened to Robbie Ducharme," I said. "I swear."

Riel looked me over carefully. Finally, he gave a little nod. He glanced at his watch.

"Supper's going to be a little late tonight," he said.

I watched him turn and head back down the hall. I heard his footsteps on the stairs, then I heard him rattling pots in the kitchen. I wondered what he was thinking. Wondered what he believed and what he suspected. Wondered, too, why I hadn't had the good sense to just stay put that night.

CHAPTER SIX

Two days later, when I went by to pick up Sal before school, I was surprised to see Vin standing on the sidewalk in front of Sal's house. I was surprised, because Vin hadn't been hanging around with Sal and me much lately. But I wasn't blown-out-of-the-water shocked because, after all, Vin lived on the next street over from Sal. You could see the back of Sal's house from the back of Vin's. At least, you could in winter, when the trees had lost their leaves.

Vin spotted me when I was still a couple of houses away. He gave a wave and started up the sidewalk toward me. He had a funny look on his face—not funny as in amused, but a strange expression, a mixture of disbelief and something that might have been worry. I wasn't sure.

"What's up?" I said.

"You kidding?" Vin said. "Up until maybe twenty minutes ago, there were five cop cars here. Five!"

I glanced up at Sal's house. The place was small, with a wooden porch that needed a paint job and a weed patch out front where there should have been a lawn. The San Miguels didn't own the place. They rented it. And they sublet the top floor to an old couple. It helped them to cover their own rent, Sal said. I couldn't imagine five people living in a house that wasn't any bigger than the one I used to live in with Billy, and that was a whole lot smaller than Riel's. Or maybe Riel's just seemed bigger because he had hardly any furniture and no clutter at all.

Sal's house was quiet. So were all the other houses up and down the street. It was hard to imagine that there had been any cop cars there, let alone five.

"What happened?" I said. I had an idea, but I wanted to find out what Vin knew.

"It was his old man," Vin said. "He got into some fight with the neighbor. My dad knows the guy. Says he's a real jerk. The guy says Sal's dad went after him with a pair of hedge clippers."

I glanced up at the house again and wondered where Sal was. The five cop cars must have drawn a lot of attention when they pulled up. There wouldn't be much chance of keeping it a secret this time. If Vin knew, then a lot of other people knew, too. People would be talking about it. Kids at school would be buzzing—*Hey, did you hear about Sal's dad? Sal's crazy dad?*

"Did they arrest him?" I asked.

"They took him away in handcuffs. Sal's mom was crying and trying to talk to them, but it all came out in

Spanish. What's the matter with the professor, Mike?" Vin always referred to Sal's dad as the professor. And even Vin thought it had to be hard for a guy to go from teaching Spanish literature and poetry in a university to cleaning office buildings. "Is he sick?"

I just shrugged. I'd made a promise to Sal. I wasn't going to break it, not even for Vin.

"Sal still home?" I asked.

Vin nodded. "Poor guy," he said. "If you ask me, his dad's really flipped. I heard someone say the reason there were five cop cars is that Sal's dad wouldn't put down the hedge clippers when the cops told him to."

Jeez, I thought. That was serious. Cops didn't like it when you were threatening someone with a weapon and refused to put it down. I looked at the house for a third time and thought about how scared Sal must have been when it was happening.

"I'd better go see how he is," I said. "You coming?"

Vin looked at the house too, his eyes big, like he thought the place might be haunted. He shook his head. "I gotta pick up Cat," he said. Then, "Hey, Mike, that new girl, what's her name, the one with the red hair?"

"Rebecca?"

Vin grinned. "Yeah. Rebecca. She's kind of cute if you like that red hair and freckles thing. I saw that look she gave you the other day. What's going on? You finally find someone to replace Jen?"

"Yeah, right," I said. I thought for a moment about which was worse—the look Jen would probably give me if we ever met face-to-face again, or the look Rebecca had given me when she came out of the school the day before yesterday. To get a glare from Jen would be worse, for sure. I cared what she thought. I didn't even know Rebecca.

"So you don't have a thing going with her?" Vin said.

"You kidding?"

"What was that look all about then?" Vin said. "A girl doesn't give that look to a guy unless she has some kind of feelings for him, right?"

"A girl doesn't give that look to a guy she has *good* feelings for," I said. "She's never even spoken to me, but she's already decided that I'm scum just because I happened to be in the wrong place at the wrong time." And I had managed that little trick twice—once in the alley and once again in the school auditorium.

"Wrong place?" Vin said.

"I overheard her talking to Riel about what she saw," I said.

"What she saw? What do you mean?"

I knew that I probably shouldn't say anything more. After all, she had been talking to Riel in confidence. Riel had made that clear enough. But she hadn't actually seen anything that could help the cops, so what did it matter? And besides, this was Vin, my best friend—well, okay, so I wasn't 100 percent sure of that right now, not with Cat in the picture. But one thing I did know: if I held out on Vin, refused to answer his question, it wouldn't help the situation. Besides, all Rebecca had seen were just kids. In the distance. Coming out of the park. Kids who maybe didn't even have anything to do with Robbie Ducharme.

There was the other thing too—the thing with the man who had identified me. A month or so ago I would have called Vin first thing to tell him all about it—because Vin was my best friend. Always had been. Probably would be again once he got over Cat.

"Mikey?"

"If I tell you," I said, "you've got to promise not to tell anyone else."

"Hey, Mike . . . " Vin gave me a wounded look, like I should know better. Best friends never ratted. Best friends never said things they shouldn't outside of the circle.

I told him about Rebecca first. "Maybe you saw it in the paper. There was a girl who said she saw kids in the park."

"Rebecca with the red hair?" Vin said.

"Yeah. But she was too far away. She couldn't ID anyone. Just knows they were kids, that's all. But that's not the best part." *Best* part? Make that *weird* part. "There was a guy too. A man. He called Crime Stoppers and said he saw a kid near the park that night. The cops showed him yearbooks from St. James, from Hillside and from our school. Guess who he ID'd?"

Vin peered intently at me and waited.

"Me," I said. I even laughed. And I guess it was kind of funny, if you looked at it the right way. "You believe that? The guy picked out my picture and told the cops I was the kid he saw near the park that night."

Vin blinked. "*You*, Mikey? You were there?"

"No," I said. "I wasn't there. That's the thing. I just happened to walk by the park that night and this guy saw me and contacted the cops. They sent a homicide detective to the house to question me and everything."

"What did you tell him?"

"Nothing. I couldn't tell him anything." Jeez, didn't Vin get it? "I wasn't there, not in the park, I mean. I just went by there."

"So you didn't see anything either," Vin said. He shook his head. "A guy gets stomped and no one sees anything. Guess the cops pretty much hit a dead end, huh?" He glanced at his watch. "If I don't get moving, Cat's gonna give me a hard time all day," he said. "That is, *if* she even speaks to me. She hates it when I'm late."

"I thought she hated it when you pretend-smoked."

"That too," Vin said. "But she's cool, Mike. If you ever got to know her, you'd like her."

I watched him go. Then I turned back to Sal's house. I had to go up there. Sal probably needed someone to talk to. And it was the right thing to do. But, man, how come the right thing always turned out to be the hard thing?

» » »

As soon as I had pressed the doorbell, I started to worry that Sal's mother would answer the door. Talking to Sal would be hard enough, but I had no idea what I would say—what I *should* say—to Mrs. San Miguel. So I was relieved when Sal's face appeared in the little diamond-shaped window cut into the inner door.

Sal peered out at me for a second, then his face disappeared. I waited. Nothing happened. Should I ring the bell again? Or should I assume that Sal didn't want to talk to me, that he probably didn't want to talk to anyone? I hesitated, trying to put myself in Sal's shoes, trying to decide what I'd want my friends to do if my dad had just been taken away in handcuffs. I decided to ring again.

The inner door opened before my finger reached the doorbell. Sal pushed open the outer aluminum door and stepped out onto the porch. He closed both doors behind himself before he said anything. When he turned around again, I saw that his eyes were watery and red around the edges. I wondered how much sleep anyone ever got at Sal's house.

"You heard about my dad, right?" Sal said.

I nodded. "Vin told me what happened."

Sal snorted. "Right. Vin. I saw him standing down there on the sidewalk. I kept waiting for him to come up to the house, but he never did."

"He probably didn't know what to say." I didn't tell Sal what I really thought, which was that if you'd known Vin for a lifetime, he could be okay, like he was when my mother died. But Sal hadn't known Vin for a lifetime. They had never been as close as Vin and I were . . . used to be . . . maybe still were. "You know Vin. You need someone to jazz you, he's the guy. You need someone to think up the right thing to say when, well, you know—Vin's not so good at that."

"Yeah," Sal said. He sounded angry. He was probably thinking the same thing I was—that if it had been important enough, Vin would have at least tried. And since he hadn't tried . . .

"You okay?" I said.

Sal nodded. His head moved up and down slowly, like it weighed as much as a boulder.

"How about your mom? How's she doing?"

"See?" Sal said. "It's not rocket science."

I blinked. "I don't get it."

"Saying the right thing. You don't have to be a genius."

Oh.

"My mom freaked out," Sal said. "At one point they all had their guns drawn. You have any idea what that's like, Mike, seeing a bunch of cops with their guns pointed at your dad? They called for a translator, but heck, it seemed to take forever. So they were telling me what to say to him and I was saying it. Then when they finally got him to drop the hedge clippers, they were all over him, pushing him down to the ground, putting handcuffs on him. You should have seen the way he looked at me. Like I was on their side or something." His voice broke and trembled. I thought maybe he was going to start to cry, but he didn't. "They took my dad away in handcuffs," he said. "And my mom started to cry and cry. It reminded her of what happened back home." Back home in Guatemala, he meant. "I called my aunt, and she called a lawyer. My mom's going down to the police station. I have to go with her. Her English isn't so good when she's upset."

"Vin said nobody got hurt," I said. "They'll probably let him come home, no problem."

Sal didn't look convinced. "There were TV cameras here," he said. "And reporters. It's going to be all over the news, I know it. So that gives my mom something else to worry about. She thinks Dad's going to lose his job."

I didn't know what to say, but I knew I should say something.

"He can't get fired for something that has nothing to do with work." That was the best I could come up with. And it was the way I thought things should work. But you never knew. I had lost the first job I ever had after I got into trouble with the police.

"It's not just that," Sal said. "When my dad gets like this, when he gets all worked up, he can't stand to be closed in, you know?"

I didn't know. Not exactly.

"He cleans those big office buildings," Sal said. "All night he's in those big high-rises. He has to ride in an elevator. Then when he gets to the offices, the windows don't open. He can't stand that. When he gets upset, he has to be outside. And if he can't get outside, then he has to have the windows open."

We stood there for a moment, not saying anything. I couldn't think of anything that would make Sal feel better. Sal just plain didn't speak.

"I'll come by after school," I said at last. "If there's any homework you need to know about, I'll let you know."

"Yeah," Sal said. His tone said it all: *Who cares about homework? What's homework going to accomplish?* "Thanks."

» » »

I dropped by Sal's after school, like I had promised, but no one answered the door. So I took out the list of homework assignments that I had collected, scribbled a note on the top of it, and shoved it through the mail slot. On the way home from Sal's place, I stopped by Blockbuster to return a video that was already a couple of days overdue. When I came out again, a car horn tooted. Riel was sitting in his car at the curb. He waved me over.

"How did you know I was here?" I said.

"I didn't," Riel said. "Get in."

"Are we going somewhere?"

"Get in, Mike."

Yes, sir. Jeez. "Seriously," I said after I buckled up, "how did you know where I was?"

Riel put the car into gear and flipped on his turn signal before pulling out into traffic. "I was looking for you."

Looking for me? That didn't sound good.

"We have to go downtown," Riel said.

"What for?"

"Detective Jones called. He wants to talk to you again."

A lump of ice formed in my stomach, its chill spreading through my whole body.

"Why?" I tried to make the word sound casual, tried to give the impression that I couldn't imagine why Detective Jones would want to talk to me again. Maybe it was nothing. Maybe he just wanted to go over my story again, maybe try to trip me up. Cop games. After all, as far as I knew, I was the only lead they had, the only kid who had been identified around the park that night. But that didn't mean anything, not if someone had only seen me walk by the park.

"He said he needed to clarify a few things," Riel said. He sounded casual enough himself, but there was a tightness around his eyes that told me that he had probably asked the same question. Any guy who used to be a detective must know what it meant when the cops wanted to talk to a person a second time.

We drove the short distance without talking. Riel parked as close as he could to police headquarters, and we went inside. He told the police officer at the front desk why we were there, then we waited for Detective Jones to come down and meet us and show us to an interview room.

"We're going to videotape this, okay, Mike?" he said.

I glanced at Riel, who nodded. I was in for it now. I

wished a bunch of things all at the same time. I wished I had never left the house that night. I wished I had never lied to Riel. The thing with lying: once you start, things can get complicated. And, boy, did I ever wish that man hadn't turned on his TV when he got back to town.

Detective Jones cautioned me again, just like he had the other day at Riel's house. And he asked me again if I understood what he had just said to me.

I nodded. I felt like an insect caught in a whirlpool. The whole room seemed to be spinning around me. Any minute now I was going to get sucked down the drain.

"Can you tell me what it means?" Detective Jones said.

My mouth was so dry that I almost choked on my answer. "It means that anything I say can be used against me," I said.

"Do you want a lawyer?" Detective Jones said. He looked at Riel.

"Let's see where you're going first," Riel said.

Detective Jones looked at me.

"Okay, Mike?"

"Okay," I said. But, boy, it was so *not* okay.

"Mike, can you tell me again where you were on the night that Robbie Ducharme was killed?"

"I already told you that." I'd told him twice. And anyway, it wasn't such a big deal.

"I know." Detective Jones's voice was calm, almost soothing. He sounded sorry to be asking the question again. But he didn't fool me. He wasn't sorry at all. He was doing his job, and his job was to find out what had happened to Robbie Ducharme. "I know we went over this already," he said, "but I need to make sure I have everything straight. Can you tell me again, Mike? Just run through it the way you remember it."

I fought down the panic that was churning up my belly the way a gale-force wind churns up lake water. Okay. No problem. I could do this. I drew in a deep breath and began. I had left the house. I had walked over to my old house. I had stood out on the street for a while, looking at the old place, thinking about Billy. Then I had taken a long walk. What had I told Detective Jones before? Oh yeah, over to Greenwood, down to Queen, east to Coxwell.

"And what time did you leave John's house?" He indicated Riel with a nod of his head.

"Around eleven," I said.

"Any idea what time you were at your old house?"

I shrugged. So far so good. I started to relax as I tried to make the calculation. It wouldn't have taken more than fifteen minutes to walk there. "Maybe quarter after," I said.

"And you stayed there how long?"

"Ten minutes. Maybe longer."

"Did you see anyone?"

I shook my head. It had always been a boring street. A street where you could count on people being safely inside at that time of night. A street where nothing much happened.

"So it was pretty quiet out there, I guess," Detective Jones said.

"Yeah, I guess."

Detective Jones sat back in his chair. If I'd had to name the expression on his face as he looked over at Riel, I would have said it was regret.

"What's your old address, Mike?"

I told him. Thirty-eight.

"Do you know what happened at thirty-four that night, Mike?"

Thirty-four? That was two houses down from where Billy and I had lived. An older couple lived there. Portuguese, I think. I didn't know their names, but the woman always used to smile at me when I went by their house and on Sundays their kids used to show up with their grandchildren, a whole pile of them.

"Mr. Cardoso," Detective Jones said. "He and his wife live at thirty-four. You know him?"

I'd seen him around. Mr. Cardoso didn't smile like his wife did. In fact, I couldn't remember ever seeing the old man smile.

"He has Alzheimer's," Detective Jones said. "You know what that is?"

Sure, I knew. "It's a disease. When you get it, you can't remember stuff."

Detective Jones nodded. "It's a degenerative brain disease. You forget all kinds of things—your past, the names of your loved ones, the streets in your own neighborhood. People who have Alzheimer's tend to wander.

They have to be watched because they can hurt themselves. They might run a bath that's all hot water, no cold, and then burn themselves badly when they get into the tub. Or they might turn on a burner on the stove and then forget all about it and burn whatever's on the stove. It can be a real fire hazard."

I got a sick feeling in my stomach. Something had happened at the Cardosos' house that night. I knew it without Detective Jones saying it. I felt like I was fighting for my life now—me against my nerves. I was fighting to stay calm, to keep my face from showing the sick feeling that was washing over me.

"Just after eleven p.m. on the night that Robbie Ducharme died, Mrs. Cardoso made a 911 call," Detective Jones said. "It seems Mr. Cardoso got out of bed sometime before that and turned on one of the gas burners on the stove. Mrs. Cardoso had made fried chicken for supper that night and she left a pan of cooking oil on the stove. You know what happens to cooking oil when it gets really hot, Mike?"

I had a pretty good idea.

"It bursts into flame," Detective Jones said. "It's a good thing Mrs. Cardoso is a light sleeper. She said she got into the habit after her husband was diagnosed with Alzheimer's. Because, let me tell you, if she hadn't woken up when she did . . . " He shrugged.

I didn't dare look at Riel, but I felt him right there at my elbow.

"What I don't understand," Detective Jones said, "is

how you could have been on your street, in front of your house, at the time you said you were, and how you didn't see the fire truck that was there. You want to tell me how that can be, Mike?"

Riel stood up abruptly. "I think I need some time with Mike," he said.

Detective Jones held his eyes on me for a moment longer. I looked at the floor. I swallowed hard and kept swallowing hard. I knew if I stopped, I'd throw up. Then Detective Jones got up and left the room.

"You let me know when you're ready," he said. I wasn't sure if he was speaking to me or Riel.

Nothing happened in the seconds after the door closed behind him. Riel was standing a little behind me and I couldn't make myself turn around to face him. I kept staring at the floor and swallowing hard. After a little while, I saw Riel's feet circle around in front of me. He pulled out a chair, positioned it directly opposite me and sat down in it.

"What's going on, Mike?" he said.

He didn't accuse me of anything. He hadn't accused me of anything the first time Detective Jones had questioned me either. What did that mean? What was Riel thinking? Jeez, what was Detective Jones thinking?

"I asked you a question, Mike," Riel said.

"I didn't have anything to do with what happened to Robbie Ducharme," I said.

"If I had to put money on it, I'd have to bet that Detective Jones thinks you did," Riel said. "He's catching you in an awful lot of lies, Mike. You lied to me about where you were that night. And then you lied to him. Lying to me, well, that's only going to make it hard for you and me to get along. But lying to the police when they're conducting a homicide investigation? That's pretty serious."

I didn't say anything. I couldn't even make myself look at Riel. I was too embarrassed, because not only had I been caught again, but now I was crying. I couldn't believe it. I was acting like a girl and I couldn't stop. I wiped angrily at the tears that were leaking out of my eyes.

"Look at me, Mike," Riel said, still in that quiet voice. It was so calm, so controlled that I almost wished he would yell. Riel reached back for something. He pressed a couple of tissues into my hand. "Blow your nose," he said. "You'll feel better."

Fat chance, but I blew anyway.

"Now look at me," Riel said.

I raised my head slowly. Riel's gray eyes were fixed on me. I didn't see anger this time. I didn't even see suspicion and disappointment. No, what I saw this time was concern. Deep concern. And it scared me more than anything else.

"If anyone asks me," Riel said, "I'm going to have to say something about what your hands looked like the next day. I'm going to have to tell them what you told me, about how you were horsing around with Sal. Then they're going to want to talk to Sal. Maybe that's not a problem. Maybe that's really what you were doing. Maybe that's exactly how it happened. But if it isn't . . . Well, if it isn't, Mike, I think the best thing is for you to tell the truth now. You lie anymore and you're only going to get yourself tangled up. You know that, right?"

I nodded.

"You think we need a lawyer here, Mike?"

We. At least he'd said *we.*

"I didn't have anything to do with Robbie Ducharme," I said. "I don't know anything about that. I swear."

"So you'll tell Detective Jones everything? Straight this time?"

I nodded again. "Yeah."

» » »

Detective Jones came back into the room. He started the video camera again. Then I told the whole story.

I said that on Tuesday evening when somehow Robbie Ducharme had ended up getting himself kicked to death in the park, I was supposed to be doing my homework. But I couldn't study. I couldn't make myself concentrate on history and math. I had been thinking about Jen. Jen who was everything I wasn't—smart, liked by all of her teachers, popular, on her way, had her pick of universities, parents well off. Jen, who was also everything I wanted. Beautiful too, with her long blond hair and her green eyes and her slim sleek body. Jen, who for some reason that I had never understood, had actually liked me. For a while there, she had maybe more than liked me.

Maybe.

How had that word crept into my thinking? It used to be that I had no question in my mind about it. Jen had liked me. She had even loved me for a while. Jen had let me kiss her and she had kissed me back. Jen came looking for me every day at school. She used to come over to my house and sit on my porch and complain about her parents. Or give me grief for not studying hard enough. She used to tell me, "You can do anything. Tell me why you *can't* do anything you put your mind to." And then Jen had met Patrick.

But I didn't say all of that to Detective Jones and the video camera. I didn't say *any* of it. Instead I said, "There's this girl I know." Correction. "*Used* to know," I said. "Jen Hayes."

Riel nodded. He knew her too.

"I went out that night to—" To what? What should I say? I went out that night to spy on her? Jeez, what would Detective Jones think? *You see, detective, I wasn't stomping Robbie Ducharme in the park. I have an alibi. I was following my former girlfriend.* That's what it would sound like. "I . . ."

Detective Jones was watching me intently.

"I knew she was going to meet someone that night. And I wanted to talk to her. And I can't call her house because her mother always answers the phone, so I . . ." I sounded pathetic. Worse than pathetic. I practically sounded like a stalker. "I wanted to see if I could talk to her."

Detective Jones didn't say anything. I glanced at Riel. He nodded, encouraging me to continue.

"I used to go out with her," I said. "And I just wanted to talk to her." I told the story carefully, not wanting to come across like a complete loser, but wanting to make sure they believed me because, right now, they didn't. Neither of them did. So I told them that I'd just wanted to talk to her, that was all. I told them that because of that, I had walked all the way down to the South Central Postal Station on Eastern Avenue. I said that I had taken care to get there before midnight—I had arrived at a quarter to—so there'd be no chance that I'd miss her. The parking lot was deserted. I didn't want to hang around in it—some security guard might see me and think I was planning to steal a car. So instead, I had stationed myself at a bus stop on the corner, where I had a good view of the parking lot, but where I wouldn't look suspicious. Then, I said, I had waited.

I said Jen had arrived a couple of minutes before midnight. I said that she had stood at one end of the parking lot for a few moments, looking around, watching for someone, and that I had ducked back into the shadows so that she wouldn't see me. I said that after that, I was afraid to peek out. I said that I kept thinking, *I'll look at her and her head will turn and she'll see me and that'll be it, she'll never speak to me again*—thinking, but not saying to Detective Jones, I'd never have another chance with her, ever, she'd never go out with me again.

I said that I had hung back in the blackness, counting off the seconds, wondering which way her pretty face was turned, dying to know who she was waiting for and why. I said that when I had finally dared another peek, I had seen only the back of her. She was getting into a car. The car pulled out the far end of the parking lot. I said that in the darkness, I couldn't make out the color of the car. I couldn't tell whether the driver was a man or a woman.

"But you're sure Jen was in the car?" Detective Jones said.

Was I sure? I formed a picture in my mind—Jen's long hair, catching a ray of overhead light or a beam of moonlight, swaying across her narrow shoulders as she ducked down into the car. Her long, slender legs, tucking themselves up into the front of the car before she tugged the door shut. I focused on that picture as I said, "Yeah, I'm sure."

"But she didn't see you?" Detective Jones said.

I shook my head.

"And the driver of the car didn't see you?"

"No. At least, I'm pretty sure."

"Did anyone at all see you there, Mike?" Detective Jones said.

I thought for a moment. "No," I said. And why would I lie about that? If anyone had seen me, I would have told the cops, right? Because if anyone had seen me, I'd have a surefire alibi. Airtight, as they always say on TV cop shows. At least, that was one way to look at it. The other way, I realized, was that no witnesses added up to not much of an alibi. I glanced at Riel. He was staring down at the table in front of him.

CHAPTER SEVEN

All the way home in the car, I kept waiting for Riel to say something, but he didn't. He drove in silence, his eyes on the traffic ahead of him and around him.

The way Detective Jones had looked at me and questioned me had scared me. It was like he thought I really had done it, or at least that I had been involved. I was scared by Riel's silence too. What was he thinking? Did he believe the same thing the police did—that somehow I was mixed up in what had happened to Robbie Ducharme? I was afraid to ask him. Afraid that he would say, "Yeah, that's exactly what I think. You did it, didn't you, Mike?" Jeez, and then what? What would happen to me?

I went up to my room and stayed there. I knew I should probably call Sal and see how he was doing, but I couldn't make myself go downstairs to get the phone. Riel was down there. I could hear the music from his stereo—old stuff, rock and roll, the kind of stuff they played on the oldies radio stations. That was all I'd heard from him ever since we'd got home. Just the music and, once in a while, footsteps from the dining room, where he sat to mark papers, to the kitchen, where the coffeemaker was. For a guy who was a major consumer of organic peanut butter and whole grain bread, Riel drank a lot of coffee.

I kept waiting for his footsteps on the stairs, kept thinking that sooner or later he was going to come into my room and stand there, filling the door frame, arms crossed over his chest, wanting to know more. Then, around midnight, the music stopped and I heard footsteps again at the bottom of the stairs, then halfway up, then at the top. I held my breath and ransacked my brain for some way to start, some way to explain everything that had happened. I had lied, there was no denying that. I had told so many lies that I felt like the kid in that story my mom had been so big on, the story about the boy who cried wolf. That was me. I had lied and lied and lied again. What could I possibly say now that would make Riel believe me?

It turned out it didn't matter.

Because when he got to the top of the stairs, Riel didn't take a right turn, which would have brought him to my room. Instead, without even hesitating, his feet went left, toward the front of the house, to his own room. I heard his door close quietly at the end of the hall. Call me a coward, but I was relieved. Relieved that

I didn't have to see that confused look in Riel's eyes, like someone had yanked a mask off my face and he was seeing me now for what I really was. But I was disappointed too. Disappointed that Riel didn't even want to talk to me, didn't want to ask me about it—jeez, didn't seem to want to waste his breath grilling me or yelling at me or lecturing me. Disappointed because he didn't seem to care. But then—and this was the killer part—why should he? How many times had I lied to him in the past few days? How many lies could a person expect to tell and still be entitled to the benefit of the doubt?

» » »

I went by Sal's house the next morning and rang the bell. No one answered. I stood on the porch for a few minutes. There were no sounds at all coming out of the house. Maybe no one was home. Maybe Sal and his family were finally getting some sleep. That would have been nice.

I walked to school alone. When I got there I kept to myself, which wasn't hard, not with Sal absent and Vin preoccupied with Cat. Just as I was leaving music class, Mr. Korchak asked me if I'd come in over lunch to reorganize the sheet music that the ninth graders were always messing up. He asked me nicely, like he knew he could count on me to take care of it for him. It made me feel a little better. Then I started to worry that Mr. Korchak was being so nice only because he hadn't heard

what was going on and that as soon as he did hear—
*You know Mike McGill? The cops have been questioning him
about Robbie Ducharme. They think he was involved.*—he'd
stop being nice to me. Who wouldn't? Still, being alone
in the music room over lunch would be better than being
in the cafeteria, surrounded by people who were griping
about what they thought were problems. You couldn't
have a worse problem than the one I had—unless you
were Robbie Ducharme.

The corridor leading to the music room was deserted. Trestles blocked off one side of it, where workmen
were still laying tile and repairing the ceiling. They had
been at it for weeks now. For a while the whole corridor
was almost completely blocked, and the only way you
could get to the music room was to make your way down
a narrow pathway between huge sheets of clear plastic
that hung from the ceiling to keep plaster and dust off
kids and teachers.

I expected the music room to be as deserted as the
hallway, so when I pushed open the door, the sound I
heard caught me off guard. It was a gasp. A whole lungful
rush of air into someone's lungs. The kind of gasp you
hear some girl make in a horror movie when she finds
herself face-to-face with Freddy Kruger or Dr. Chuck-
les. The sound came from Rebecca-with-the-red-hair.
It came out of her at the exact second that she turned
away from the music that was sitting on a stand in front
of her and toward the door to see who was there. When
she gasped, her eyes almost popped out of her head and

she jumped to her feet, clutching her instrument—tenor saxophone, the same instrument I played. She was so rattled that she knocked over her music stand, sending her sheet music sliding across the floor. It came to rest at my feet.

"What are you doing here?" she said. Said? Demanded, like the music room was her own private room, like, how dare I show up here!

I thought about saying some wiseass thing to her. Or maybe just ignoring her—she didn't have the right to ask me that. Maybe I would have too, if it wasn't for what I saw in her coppery eyes. You couldn't miss it, anymore than you could miss the wild way her eyes searched behind me, like she was looking for, maybe hoping for, even *praying* for, someone to come to her rescue. The force of that expression pushed me back a pace.

"Mr. Korchak asked me to clean up here over lunch," I said. I said it quietly, the way you'd talk to a stray kitten you were trying to lure to a saucer of milk. I hardly even knew Rebecca, but there I was, working hard at conveying a simple message: *Don't be afraid.*

She kept her eyes on me as she removed the mouthpiece from her saxophone, tucked it into its case and then into her backpack. Her eyes were still on me while she put the sax back into its own case. It was as if she didn't dare look away from me because she was afraid I'd do something to her. But what? What did she think I was going to do? She didn't know me, so who was she to decide I was someone she had to be afraid of? Who was she to pass judgment on me? And that's when I got mad.

I stepped farther into the room. All I was going to do was pick up the sheet music she had dropped. That's what I was here for, right? I was here because Mr. Korchak had trusted me to clean up the place.

Rebecca didn't just move back. She *leaped* back, like I was a foaming-at-the-mouth killer dog, and if she didn't move fast she was going to be a goner. I saw another flash of panic in her eyes when she realized that she'd just jumped farther from the door, farther from escape.

Jeez.

I snatched up the sheet music that she'd dropped and held it up over my head, like a white flag. Then, so she'd get the point, I backed away from the door. She fumbled for her backpack, still not taking her eyes off me, like she was afraid that if she did, I'd pick exactly that moment to attack. But *why?* That's what I didn't get. Why was she so afraid of me? Or was she this jumpy around everyone? She'd seen kids come out of the park. She'd said she couldn't identify them. She didn't even know what school they were from. She was new around here and didn't know many people. So, okay, I guess I could see she might be afraid that someone had seen her. Maybe she'd been standing under a streetlight. I bet that red hair of hers would have burned like flame in its beam. Okay, I could understand that. But I knew for a fact that I would never hurt her. I would never hurt anyone if I could help it. So it bugged me that she was treating me like I was some kind of crazed killer.

She grabbed her backpack by the loop at the top of it and fled for the door. She didn't even stop to sling a strap over her shoulder. I heard her footsteps running down the corridor.

» » »

Riel was home when I got back from school. I didn't see him, but I heard him in the kitchen, talking on the phone.

"I don't know," he was saying. "I don't think it's a good idea to leave him to his own devices right now."

Him. He meant me. He was talking about me.

"I don't know," Riel said again. Then, "Yeah, maybe. Yeah." Silence. "Okay. Later, then."

The telephone handset clunked down onto the cradle. I headed for the stairs, fast. I didn't want to face him. I was halfway to the top when he called me.

I forced a smile onto my face to try to hide what I was feeling. It wasn't so much that I was scared as that I was, well, *uncertain*, I guess. When Riel had agreed to take me in, we'd had an understanding. I understood that he was going to be strict, but I also understood that was because he had this idea that I could turn out all right if I took school seriously, got a job, and started to think about my future. And he understood that just because I'd had problems in the past, that didn't mean my life was over. At least, that's what he told me he under-stood. I wondered if he was still operating on that basis, or if he'd done a serious rethink of where he thought I was headed.

I turned around to face him.

"You have any plans for tonight?" Riel said. He was dressed completely in black, his favorite color. It made him look even taller than he was, and scarier.

I shrugged. The dance was tonight, the one Sal had bugged me to buy a ticket for. But I didn't feel like going, and it was a safe bet that Sal had other things besides dancing on his mind. If this were an ordinary Friday night, I probably would have done something with Vin. But Vin had his new interests and new friends. So, no, I didn't have any plans.

"I was thinking of taking Susan out for dinner," Riel said. "Can I trust you to stay here and stay out of trouble?"

I'd heard the question before. Almost every time Riel went out with Susan, he asked it. Usually he was smiling when he said it, kidding me a little, for sure never giving me the impression that he had any reservations about going out and leaving me alone. Usually. Tonight, though, he wasn't smiling. His eyes were fixed fast on me. Tonight he seemed to want something more than a simple yes. A blood oath, maybe.

"Yeah," I said. "I was just going to watch TV."

"Not planning to go out?"

I shook my head. Firmly. Without a second's hesita-tion. Because I knew that was what he wanted.

"I might be back late," Riel said. "I'll check in with you, okay?"

Meaning, I'll check *on* you.

"No problem," I said.

» » »

I waited all weekend for the phone to ring or for the big knock to come on the door. I don't know why, but I was sure it was going to happen. Probably because I thought I deserved it after all the lies I had told. I got the shakes every time I heard the phone ring. A couple of times I had trouble catching my breath.

But the cops didn't call. They didn't come to the house either, sirens blaring, to slap the cuffs on me and haul me off to jail. In fact, nothing at all happened. And no news is good news, right? That's what my mom used to say. Mostly she'd say it when she had gone to an interview for a new job and was waiting to see if they'd call her and say, "Congratulations, Ms. McGill, you're hired!" Her thinking was, sure, they hadn't said yes, but they hadn't said no either, so maybe they were still considering her.

So, if I wanted to, I could take the same positive view of things. I could tell myself that the reason I was still at liberty was that they hadn't been able to find anything against me. The reason I wasn't locked up somewhere was that I was in the clear. I could tell myself, never mind David Milgaard, Donald Marshall, and Rubin

Carter, the cops never got it wrong. Or, at least, they wouldn't get it wrong in my case. In fact, that *is* what I told myself. I even tried to believe it.

» » »

Riel was standing in the hall near my locker after school on Monday. His expression was grim.

"Get your stuff," he said. "We need to talk."

"Is something wrong?" I said. Yeah, give me a gold shield and call me detective. Like it took more than three brain cells in total to figure out the answer to that question. If Riel was waiting for me at my locker—something he had never, ever done before—then something was wrong. Very wrong.

"Just get your stuff, Mike."

I was sure Riel being here and being in such a sour mood had something to do with the cops. But I didn't ask because there were a lot of kids in the hall, stashing books in their lockers and stuffing notebooks and binders into their backpacks. So I did the same thing. I shoved the books I didn't need up onto the top shelf of my locker and crammed the books I did need into my backpack. When I turned around, shouldering my load—*Don't make a paperback textbook when you can add a few pounds to the daily load by slapping hard covers on them, right?*—I saw Cat a couple of lockers down, watching me. Riel didn't seem to notice. He nudged me to get me moving.

"What's wrong?" I said.

"Later," Riel said. It was all he said. He walked to the stairs and went down them quickly, checking every few steps to make sure that I was with him. If I was a pace or two behind, he looked impatient. Well, tough. If he wanted me to power on the speed, then the least he could do was tell me what the problem was.

We went through the front door of the school and out onto Gerrard Street. A streetcar stood at the corner, in the westbound track. Both the front and rear doors were open, which meant that it was illegal for cars to pass it. A double line of cars stretched back more than a block behind it. Ahead of it, the traffic light was green. Another streetcar jam-up, I figured. Another normal day in Toronto. It was no big deal. Nothing I would have paid attention to at all if it weren't for the fact that I saw Sal standing on the back steps of the streetcar, holding the door open.

A car behind the streetcar honked its horn. Then, like little children catching onto a fun idea, the drivers of other cars started to lean on their horns. Sal didn't move from the steps.

"What's Sal up to?" Riel said.

I shook my head and started to walk toward the streetcar. When I got closer, I heard Sal speaking to someone in Spanish. His hand was stretched out, reaching for his father, who was standing at the top of the streetcar steps. Inside, the streetcar driver was saying, "Get on or get off, it's all the same to me. But do something so that I can get this vehicle moving."

Sal spoke again, quietly but urgently. I saw him try to grab his father's hand. His father ducked back out of his way but didn't get off the streetcar steps.

"Look, mister, if you don't move, I'm going to have to call the cops," the driver said.

"No," Sal said. "No, it's okay. Don't call them. He's fine. He just can't breathe, that's all."

"There's plenty of air outside," the driver said.

"Maybe a window seat," Sal said. "With the windows open."

I glanced along the length of the streetcar. All of the window seats were taken and all of the windows were closed against the chilly air. Nobody looked like they wanted to move to make room for a man who was delaying their trip. Then someone shouted. It took a moment for me to understand that it was Sal's dad. He yelled something, and I saw him run up the aisle toward the driver. Sal jumped up into the streetcar and ran after him. I could hear him talking fast, but softly, to his dad. He caught his father by the hand and led him to the back door of the streetcar again. But once they got to the door, Sal's dad stood his ground. He jerked his hand away from Sal.

"That's it," the driver said. He appeared at the door right behind Sal's dad. "That's it, I'm calling the cops."

I looked back up at Sal and saw the panic in his face. After everything that had been happening, he didn't want the police anywhere near his dad.

"Just a minute, sir, if you don't mind," said a voice behind me. Riel's voice. He was talking to the driver. "I know this man. Just give me a minute." Then he turned to Sal and said, "Ask your father if he'd like a ride home. Tell him he can ride up front and we'll keep all the windows open."

Sal's face flooded with gratitude when he turned to look at Riel. His expression changed, though, when he saw me.

"Ask him," Riel said, his voice gentle and encouraging.

Sal spoke in Spanish to his father and held out his hand again. Riel stepped closer to Sal and said something I didn't understand, because it was in Spanish. I stared at him. But Sal's father came down out of the streetcar.

"Thank you," Riel said to the streetcar driver. Then he said something else in Spanish. Sal gave me a look that said, *How come you never told me?* All I could do was shrug.

Riel's car was parked just down the street from the school, which surprised me. Most of the time he walked to school. "It's good for you," he always said. If he drove—which he did when he had a lot of stuff to carry or when he knew he was going to have to run errands at the end of the day—he parked in the staff parking lot. I wondered why he hadn't done that today.

The first thing Riel did after he unlocked the car was roll down all the windows. Then he came around to the passenger side and opened the door for Sal's dad, who was standing on the sidewalk. Riel looked at me like, what was I waiting for? I climbed into the backseat with Sal.

Sal told Riel his address. Riel drove to Sal's house, talking to Sal's dad in Spanish all the way. Riel did most of the talking. Except for a word here and there, the most Sal's dad did was nod. Mostly he looked straight ahead. His head was leaning toward the open window. I was worried that he was going to stick his head right out, but he didn't.

When Riel pulled up in front of Sal's house, Sal got out and opened the door for his father. Mr. San Miguel got out. If he thanked Riel for the ride, I didn't hear him. He just walked up the little path to the porch and disappeared inside. As I was getting out of the back seat to go and sit up front with Riel, Sal leaned down through the open passenger door and said, "Thanks, Mr. Riel. I was afraid the driver was going to call the cops."

"I'm glad I could help," Riel said. Then he said, "Is your mother holding up okay?"

Sal shrugged. "My aunt comes over a lot."

"How about you?"

Sal looked down, away from Riel. He did the same thing whenever a girl he liked looked at him. It meant he was embarrassed.

"I'm okay," he said. "Thanks."

Sal glanced at me as he straightened up and turned toward his house. His eyes were all watery again. He sucked in a deep breath, slung one strap of his backpack over his shoulder, and marched up the front path like a guy marching into battle. I guess, in a way, that that was exactly what he was doing.

I slid into the front seat and fastened the seatbelt.

"I didn't know you could speak Spanish," I said.

"I spent some time traveling in Latin America," Riel said, "while I was trying to decide what to do with my life. I wanted to meet girls. And after I met a few—" He shrugged. "If anyone ever tells you that the best way to learn a language is to go out with a girl who speaks it, they're not lying to you, Mike. Trust me."

The thought of Riel being tutored by a pretty Spanish-speaking girl made me smile. It also made me think about what I would do when I finished high school.

Instead of heading home, Riel drove down to Queen Street. He parked the car and led me into his favorite restaurant, which from the outside looks like a hole in the wall. Inside, though, the place is clean and cheerful. Better than that, it serves the best burgers and the best ribs I've ever tasted. Maybe that's why Riel liked it so much. Or maybe he liked it because all the waitresses knew him and seemed to enjoy flirting with him, even the married ones.

Riel led the way to a booth in the back. He ordered coffee, then looked over at me. I ordered a Coke. Riel didn't say anything while Annette, the waitress, went to get our drinks. That made me nervous all over again. Whatever Riel wanted to talk to me about, it was serious.

Annette set a mug of coffee and a small bowl of plastic creamers in front of Riel and a large Coke in front of me. Riel pulled the foil lid off one of the creamers and dumped the contents into his mug. He stared down at his coffee while he stirred it. When he put down his spoon, he looked directly at me.

"Jonesy wants to see you again," he said. "You have any idea why?"

I shook my head. But I guessed that if Detective Jones wanted to see me again, it had to be something about Robbie Ducharme.

"We've got an appointment downtown," Riel said. "I asked a friend of mine to meet us there. A lawyer."

Part of me wanted to laugh—nice try, ha-ha, but you can't scare me. Another part of me felt cold and numb. A lawyer. That must mean that Riel thought it was serious too.

"Why would he want to see me again?" I asked.

Riel wrapped his hands around his mug of coffee. So far he hadn't taken even one sip. "Mike, if there's anything I should know, anything you want to tell me, anything at all, now would be a good time to speak up."

It felt like all of the air had been sucked out of the little restaurant. I had to breathe hard to fill my lungs. The bright sunny lighting faded to a dull gray. I saw Riel's lips moving and knew that he was saying something else to me, but the words were drowned out by the hammering of my heart. Did Riel think I hadn't told the truth about that night, about Jen? Did he still think I was lying? Is that why he'd said that?

"Mike?"

I looked up at him and swallowed hard. If the cops wanted to talk to me again, it couldn't be good. If they'd just wanted to say that my story had checked out, no problem, they would have told Riel. And for sure Riel wouldn't be sitting across from me with the same expression on his face that my mother used to have when she got another call from Billy's school saying Billy had ditched classes again.

"I told you the truth," I said. Please believe me. *Please.* "The whole truth."

Riel peered at me. After a while he nodded. Maybe I would have felt better if he had nodded sooner or if he hadn't looked like he'd just been fired, or like Susan had dumped him.

"Drink up," Riel said.

But I didn't touch my Coke. Riel threw a couple of dollars onto the table. He hadn't touched his coffee either.

» » »

Riel's lawyer friend was named Rhona Katz. She was tall and thin and pretty—Riel seemed to know a lot of pretty women. She had on a pale blue skirt with a matching jacket. The color reminded me of my mother's eyes. She smelled nice too, the way my mother used to. She was standing outside police headquarters, holding an expensive-looking leather briefcase. She smiled when she saw Riel and shifted her briefcase from her right hand to her left so that she could shake my hand when she introduced herself. Her grip was firm. So was her voice as she told me that the best thing for me to do was answer all of the questions the police wanted to ask. But, she said, if anything came up that I wasn't sure about or that I wanted to talk to her about first, I should just say so. Then she said, "Is there anything you want to tell me before we go up, Mike?" She looked and sounded casual as she said it, and at first I thought it was a routine lawyer question, something she always asked. Then I caught her exchanging glances with Riel.

"There's nothing," I said. "I already told John." Meaning Riel. "I told the truth."

She didn't argue with me. She just nodded and said, "That's fine."

Detective Jones looked a lot more serious than the last time I had seen him, which was really saying something. His partner, Detective London, was with him. I'd met him before, when Billy had died. Detective London eyed me like I was a three-egg, five-slices-of-bacon breakfast and he hadn't eaten in days.

"Sit down, Mike," Detective Jones said.

I sat.

"Tell me again where you were the night Robbie Ducharme was killed," he said.

"Suppose *you* tell me why you're asking," Rhona Katz said.

Detective Jones glanced at her for all of a nanosecond before turning back to me. "Mike?"

Rhona Katz laid a hand on my arm.

"It's okay," I said. I was going to convince him this time. I was going to convince them all. I told him again when I had left the house, why I'd left, exactly where I'd gone, what I'd done and when I had returned home.

"And you never spoke to Jen Hayes that night," Detective Jones said. "And, as far as you know, she didn't know you were there and she didn't see you. Is that right?"

I nodded.

"Pretty convenient," Detective London said. Something in his tone made me look at him. He stared right back at me like I was every bad kid he had ever come across—a liar, a cheat, a thief, and 100 percent not to be trusted.

"Detective," Rhona Katz said, "unless you have something concrete—"

Detective Jones kept his eyes hard on me the whole time. He didn't smile at me anymore, didn't try to sound friendly, didn't talk softly to encourage me. "We spoke to Jen," he said. "She says she was with her best friend Ashley Tierney that night."

Jeez. That was the one thing I hadn't counted on. I tried to keep my face neutral, but Detective Jones seemed to pick up on something.

"But you knew that already, didn't you, Mike?" he said.

I stared down at the tabletop. I didn't answer. I was thinking about Jen. Thinking about the cops going to her school or her house and asking to talk to her. Imagined them saying, *"It's about Mike McGill. He says he saw you on Tuesday night. He says . . ."* I thought about the look on Jen's face, and then immediately tried to shake the picture that formed in my mind.

"Ashley and Jen say they were together *all night*," Detective Jones said. "They were at Ashley's house from a little after six in the evening until the next morning. Jen slept over because they were doing an English presentation together the next morning."

Jen, walking up the path to Ashley's house with her backpack and the little suitcase she used when she was sleeping over at a friend's house.

"You spoke with Ashley's parents too?" Rhona Katz said.

"They're divorced," Detective Jones said. "Ashley lives with her mother—who was home all night."

"And who can testify under oath that Jen Hayes never left her house that night?" Rhona Katz said.

"Mrs. Tierney never left the house," Detective Jones said, not exactly answering the question.

"That's a no," Riel said to Rhona Katz. "Ten to one Mrs. Tierney will say the girls were in Ashley's room all night. Or that she was in *her* room all night. Am I right, Jonesy?"

Detective Jones looked annoyed. "Ashley's pretty firm—she insists that Jen was with her all night."

"You did say *best* friends, didn't you?" Rhona Katz said.

Detective Jones glanced at his partner. Detective London said, "You want to tell us about how you got those marks on your knuckles, Mike?"

I looked down at my hands. They were pretty well healed. You had to look close to notice that anything had been wrong with them.

"You told John that you got your hands banged up when you were horsing around with your friend Salvatore San Miguel, right?" Detective Jones said.

My cheeks felt like they were on fire. Riel had spoken to them about me. He'd told them stuff about me and he hadn't let me know.

"That came as a big surprise to Sal," Detective Jones said.

They'd spoken to Sal too? Why hadn't Sal said anything? If the cops had come around asking me questions about Sal, for sure I would have told him. Then I remembered the look on his face when Riel and I had appeared at the streetcar door. He had been relieved to see Riel, but he hadn't looked quite so happy that I was there. At the time I thought he was embarrassed at me seeing his father acting so weird, but now I knew that wasn't it at all. At least, it wasn't the whole story.

"I was mad," I said. I had been mad then and, boy, was I ever mad now. Mad at Sal. Mad at Jen. Mad at everyone who was making me look bad. "I went all the way down there so I could talk to Jen and then it just didn't work out. I punched a wall."

"Why did you lie to John about it, Mike?" Detective Jones asked.

"Or are you lying now?" Detective London said.

"Okay, that's it," Rhona Katz said. She started to stand up.

"One more question," Detective London said.

Rhona Katz sat down again, but only on the edge of her seat this time, like she was ready to leave the room at any moment.

Detective London leaned in close to me. His eyes were hard. His breath hit my face like a warm breeze. It smelled of onions. "Did you and Robbie Ducharme ever go at it?" he said.

I glanced at Riel, who was frowning now. Riel, who had spent some time in homicide. Who knew how it worked. Who knew when they asked certain questions and how and why and what they knew or thought they knew before they asked.

"And Mike?" Detective Jones said. "The truth this time." He emphasized the last two words, making it seem that I had been lying every other time.

"No," I replied. "We never *went at it*." I used the same words that Detective London had, spitting each one at him.

"You're sure about that, Mike?" Detective Jones said. His tone went all soft now. He asked the question in a friendly tone, the way I might ask Vin, Did she let you kiss her? And I got it. He was supposed to be the good cop. His partner was the bad cop. "You told John you didn't know Robbie, isn't that right, Mike?"

"I said he was in my math class. I said he wasn't my friend, though."

"You also said you never talked to him. Is that true, Mike?"

I swallowed hard. I didn't dare look at Riel now. Why was he asking me this? What did he know?

"Mike? Is it true you never talked to Robbie Ducharme?"

I took a deep breath. I'd promised myself I wouldn't lie anymore. But telling the truth wasn't going to help me either. It wasn't going to help because it wasn't 100 percent true that I had never exchanged a word with Robbie Ducharme. It wasn't 100 percent true, either, that Robbie Ducharme was just a big empty zero to me, the way I'd let Riel think. It wasn't 100 percent true that I didn't know anything or care anything about Robbie. That is, it hadn't been 100 percent true recently. But it *had* more or less described my feelings about Robbie right up until what had happened to Billy. Then, for some reason that I still didn't understand, Robbie Ducharme had actually decided to talk to me. And what he'd said was something that I hadn't wanted to hear.

I had been walking down the hall at school one day. This was back when I was living in temporary foster care, back when Riel was still being checked out. Robbie and I had probably passed each other in the hall a thousand times. Probably most of those times we hadn't even noticed each other. For sure we had never spoken to each other. It was after school. The halls were quiet. Some of them were deserted. I had stayed back in music—the one subject I liked—to help Mr. Korchak do his weekly tidy-up. I stayed at school as late as I could in those days. The temporary foster care was okay. The woman, Mrs. Walsh, was nice enough, but she was in charge of three other kids, all of them younger than me. One was a girl who cried pretty much every night. The other two were nine-year-old twins who kicked anyone who came near them. They were in therapy, Mrs. Walsh said. She was sure they'd be fine, she said. She was also sure that Teresa, the girl who cried all the time, would eventually find something to smile about. If I'd pressed her for an opinion—which I hadn't—Mrs. Walsh probably would have told me that she was sure I'd be fine too.

"Life throws us a curve every now and then," she'd said to me when I first arrived at her place. "But in my experience, if you hang in there, she'll throw some right over the plate too, and if you're ready, you'll hit a few home runs."

She was nice enough. I guess she meant well too, but, boy, she'd have had to be a million times nicer to make me want to race back to her place the minute the final bell rang to get kicked in both shins at the same time by the terror twins while I listened to Teresa cry.

I had finished in the music room and was heading for my locker when I saw Robbie Ducharme coming toward me. Great big zero math-brainer Robbie Ducharme. Only instead of passing by with his mouth shut like he usually did, Robbie stopped in front of me. He glanced up and down the hall, maybe to make sure we were alone, that it was just the two of us. Then he stood there with his mouth hanging open, like he was breathing through it, until he got on my nerves, which didn't take long.

"What's your problem?" I said.

And Robbie—I still couldn't believe that he'd actually said it or that he'd even thought he had the right to say it, that he thought it was *any* of his business— Robbie said, "I wouldn't cry for someone who did what your uncle did."

I stared at Robbie's eyes, big and blue and blurry behind the lenses of his glasses. I looked at his heavy, doughy body. He was the kind of guy who spent all of his spare time in front of a computer or a math book, not outside kicking a ball around or rollerblading or playing a little pickup softball.

"Who you cry over says everything," Robbie said.

What did he mean by that? And why was he talking about crying? Sure, I had cried at Billy's funeral. So what? Even after what he had done, he was still my uncle. He'd looked after me. Well, sort of. And, okay, there was that time a while back when a couple of guys had given me a hard time over Billy. I'd hit one of them and he'd hit me back and, yeah, maybe I'd cried—a *little*—and had been embarrassed because there was a whole crowd of people watching. But so what? What did that have to do with Robbie Ducharme? What did he even know about me? What did he know about Billy except what he might have read in the paper or seen on TV—or heard about at school? Sure, everybody had talked about it after it had happened, but nobody except Vin and Sal had known Billy. No one had known what he was really like.

Still, I was prepared to walk right past Robbie Ducharme, no harm done. I was prepared to mind my own business even if Robbie couldn't do the same. But Robbie wouldn't let me. He grabbed me and said, "If your mother had seen you, what would she think?"

That was when I shoved him. Hard. As hard as I could. The idea—I thought about it later, a *lot*—wasn't so much to hurt Robbie as it was to get him as far away from me as possible. I didn't punch him. I didn't swing and connect with his belly or his chubby face. I just shoved him. Was it my fault that he couldn't control his own body, that he was probably the most uncoordinated guy on the planet? Was it my fault that he couldn't do what any two-year-old could do, which is regain his balance and stay upright?

Robbie staggered backward. Then it looked to me like his feet got tangled up in each other, because the next moment he wasn't staggering. Instead he was falling. His hands flew out to each side to try to grab onto something, but there was nothing to grab. He hit the floor butt-first. Then his back made contact. Then his head whacked the ground. It bounced up again, like a basketball, hung a little above the floor for a split second, then slammed back down. I heard a *crack*, an *oomph*, a groan. Robbie didn't move.

I didn't move either. I stood exactly where I had been standing when I had shoved him, and I thought one thing and one thing only: *Jeez, I hope he's not dead.* Because that could happen, right? A guy takes a bad fall or whacks his head hard enough, and that's all she wrote.

I stared at Robbie, who looked like a big chunky mannequin lying there on the floor. Then I noticed that his chest was rising and falling. That meant he was breathing. That was a good thing. Then his eyes opened. One of his hands came up to his face to adjust his glasses, which had been knocked sideways when he fell. I thought about helping him up, but I couldn't make myself touch him. Also, I didn't want to make a move until I had scoped out the situation.

Robbie's legs twitched. He groped the floor with his hands and maneuvered himself into a sitting position. He was sniffling. I peered at him. Wouldn't you know it? Robbie Ducharme was crying.

"Nice," said a voice somewhere behind me. I spun to face a girl whose locker was in the same bank as mine. I didn't know much about her then except that the kids all called her Cat. That's what she reminded me of. A sleek, satisfied cat, purring away. She was standing in the hall with a bunch of her friends, and they were all looking at Robbie. I wondered when they'd arrived and how much they had seen.

"Nice going," Cat said. "Beating up on the fat kid with glasses. Classy move." As far as I could tell, she wasn't being sarcastic.

I turned and walked down the hall, forcing myself to move slowly, *not* to run, no way was I going to run.

I spent the whole of the following day convinced that I was going to be called down to the office and suspended or expelled or worse. Maybe Mr. Gianneris would call it assault and maybe he'd call the cops on me. But absolutely nothing happened. Robbie must have decided—finally—to keep his mouth shut. Cat must have decided not to say anything either. The same with her friends. I tried to forget the whole thing. I mean, *I* knew I hadn't been trying to hurt Robbie. But to anyone watching, it was what Cat said, me beating up on the fat kid with glasses. So I never said anything about it to anyone, not even Vin. But somebody had sure said something recently. And I'd have bet my life that they'd said it to good old Jonesy.

"Well?" Detective Jones said now. "Is it true, Mike? Is it true that you never talked to Robbie Ducharme?"

I shook my head. I didn't look at Riel, but I sure imagined the look on his face.

"Did you talk to Robbie about six weeks ago, Mike?" Detective Jones said.

I swallowed hard. No matter what I said now, they were going to think I'd been lying before. They were going to think I'd been trying to hide something. They all were—even Riel.

"It's no big deal," I said.

"What's no big deal?" Detective Jones said.

"He—Robbie—he made a crack about my uncle."

"And that made you angry, didn't it, Mike?" Detective Jones said. "Did it make you want to get even with Robbie?"

Rhona Katz put a hand on my arm. "You don't have to answer," she said.

Sure, I could have kept quiet. Taken the fifth if we'd had a fifth for me to take. *I refuse to answer on the grounds that it might incriminate me.* That would make me look great.

I don't know where, but I finally found enough courage to turn and look at Riel. The minute I did, I wished I hadn't. The expression on his face was grim. He met my eyes but didn't say anything. Boy, if he didn't think it before, for sure he thought it now. He thought I'd been lying to him. He probably thought I'd started way back the morning after Robbie was killed and that I'd never stopped. Well, why not? The truth was, I *had* been lying. I had told Riel that I was home when really I had sneaked out of the house. I had told him I'd hurt my knuckles horsing around with Sal when that wasn't true either. I had said I'd never spoken to Robbie Ducharme when a bunch of kids had seen me do worse. If I clammed up now, if I refused to answer, that would be it for Riel. He'd never believe me again.

"I shoved him," I said finally. "He made some stupid comment about my uncle and my mother, and I got mad and I shoved him. That's all."

Out of the corner of my eye, I saw Riel slump in his chair.

"And what about a week ago Monday?" Detective Jones said.

I didn't understand the question. Why was he asking me about a week ago Monday—exactly two weeks ago now?

"What about it?" I said.

"Did you talk to Robbie Ducharme a week ago Monday?"

I shook my head. I couldn't remember even seeing Robbie a week ago Monday.

"You didn't talk to him outside the music room at your school?" Detective Jones said.

"No," I said. Where had he got that idea?

"You're sure?" Detective Jones continued questioning. "You didn't see Robbie, maybe talk to him a bit? Maybe you were still mad at him for what he said about your uncle. I know how you felt about Billy, Mike. And Robbie didn't know the whole story, did he? He didn't understand about Billy. Look, Mike, it's normal to get angry when somebody makes a crack about someone who's important to you. And sometimes when that happens, you lose your temper. That's normal too. It happens to everybody. So maybe you lost your temper, maybe you were mad at Robbie and things got out of hand. If that's what happened, Mike, you can tell us. Is that what happened?"

"Mike," Rhona Katz said, "you don't have to—"

"I didn't even see Robbie that Monday," I said.

"You're sure about that, Mike?"

I nodded. Okay, so maybe I hadn't told the whole truth so far. But, jeez, I hadn't done anything to seriously hurt Robbie Ducharme either.

For a few seconds it was completely silent in the room. Then Detective Jones leaned forward a little. He said, "Somebody saw you with him, Mike."

"I'm not talking about passing him in the hall, Mike," Detective Jones said. He sounded patient. "Mike, do you know Catherine Phillips?"

Catherine Phillips? I shook my head.

"Her friends call her Cat," Detective Jones said.

Oh. Cat. "Sure. I know her."

"What would you say, Mike, if I told you that Catherine told us that she saw you and Robbie together outside the music room after school on the Monday before Robbie was killed?" Detective Jones said.

What?

"It's not true," I said. "I wasn't anywhere near the music room after school that day."

"No? Can you tell us where you were?"

A week ago Monday? After school? Had I hooked up with Sal? I tried to remember. Yeah, that's what I must have done. I must have hooked up with Sal. It's what I did most days. We'd meet and we'd walk up the hill together and hang out, maybe get a Slurpee at 7–Eleven before I started work.

"I guess I must have met my friend Sal. We walk partway home together."

Detective Jones glanced at Riel. They both had the same look in their eyes—disappointment—but probably not for the same reason.

"Mike," the detective said, "we talked to Sal, remember?"

What did that mean? Had Sal said that he wasn't with me after school that day? Okay, so maybe Sal's memory was as sharp as Mr. Brown's and mine was as dull as the rusty knife that I felt ripping into my guts.

"Then I must have gone directly to my job," I said.

"Your job doesn't start until four o'clock," Detective Jones said. "And your former employer says you were late that day. He says you didn't show up until much later, nearly four-thirty."

"That's not true," I said. I was never late for work. Boy, I could just imagine it. The cops go and talk to Mr. Kiros. And Mr. Kiros, who already thinks I've been stealing from him and letting all my friends steal from him, *he* tries to think back almost two whole weeks and—what do you know?—he can remember that. *Yeah, now that you mention it, officer, that boy came in late that day.* I wouldn't have been surprised if he'd rattled on about how I was stealing him blind too. "I wasn't late for work that day," I said.

Detective Jones's gaze was steady. "So you remember that you got to your job on time that day," he said. "But you don't remember that you weren't with your friend Sal and you don't remember where you actually were. You see the problem here, don't you, Mike?"

I had to fight off another panic attack. Detective Jones wasn't understanding me. And because he wasn't understanding, he was making it look like I was hiding something.

"What I mean," I said, "is that I know it's not true that I was late for work because I was never late for work," I said. "Mr. Kiros's wife was late all the time. She was supposed to relieve me at six, but she never showed up on time." I looked at Riel for confirmation. "But I was never late," I said.

Detective London was shaking his head. "So you're saying Mr. Kiros is lying, is that it, Mike?"

I nodded. He had to be.

"Why would he do that, Mike?"

"He doesn't like me."

Detective London rolled his eyes. "What we have here, Mike, is that your friend Sal says you weren't with him that day," he said. "Your former boss says you showed up late for work that day. And Catherine Phillips says she saw you and Robbie Ducharme together outside the music room right after school—when you weren't with your friend Sal and you weren't at work and you say you can't remember where you were. You want to know what else she says, Mike?"

What *else?* What else could she possibly have said? I hadn't been outside the music room with Robbie Ducharme a week ago Monday. So what else could she have told the cops?

"She says she saw Robbie pass you in the hall. She says you went out of your way to bump into him. Does that sound about right, Mike? She says Robbie backed away immediately. She says it looked like he was afraid of you, on account of what happened the first time. Is that right, Mike? Was he afraid of you? Did he have a good reason to be? Because Catherine says you threatened him. She says *she* was afraid you were going to hurt him again."

"*What?*" That wasn't possible. "I didn't threaten Robbie. Why would I do that?"

"Because you were still mad at him," Detective London said, like I was some kind of idiot, like he had to spell it out for me in a loud voice. "You're the kind of guy who loses his temper, right, Mike? The kind of guy who uses his fists when he's angry."

"Okay," Rhona Katz said. This time she stood up and didn't sit down again. "That's it. Unless you have something definite that ties my client to the incident in the park, we're out of here."

"Come on, Mike," Detective Jones said. He peered into my eyes and wouldn't stop. He looked like he felt sorry for me. "Why don't you just tell us what happened? Get it over with. You'll feel better. Everybody feels better when they've made a clean breast of it. What happened? Did you just happen to run into Robbie in the park? Did he say something about your Uncle Billy again? Is that what happened?"

"Come on, Mike," Rhona Katz said. She touched my arm.

I was amazed that my legs were strong enough to hold me. I pushed back my chair with trembling hands and followed her to the door. Riel was right behind me.

I don't remember how I got from the interview room to the sidewalk next to Riel's car. But there I was, standing on the sidewalk while Rhona Katz said, "We need to talk." There I was, watching Riel make an appointment with her for the next morning and then watching Rhona

Katz step out into the street to flag a cab while Riel circled to the driver's side of his car and unlocked the door.

I got in and buckled my seatbelt.

"I didn't do it," I said. "I never threatened Robbie Ducharme outside the music room. And I didn't see him in the park. Except for that time I shoved him, I never touched him."

Riel sat still, his hands gripping the steering wheel, his eyes focused forward. He sat like that for a while before slipping a key into the car's ignition. Before he started the car, he looked hard at me and said, "Somebody sure isn't telling the truth."

I didn't have the courage to ask Riel who he thought that somebody was.

» » »

For the first time that I could remember, Riel didn't cook supper. Instead he ordered in pizza. As far as I could tell, it wasn't organic.

We sat at the table in the kitchen, Riel opposite me, the open pizza box between us. Riel worked his way through a piece, chewing on it as enthusiastically as if it were a piece of cardboard. He washed down each mouthful with a gulp of beer straight from the bottle. I was usually good for half a large pizza, but not tonight. I nibbled at the one slice on my plate.

Riel drained the last of the beer from the bottle in front of him. "Remember I told you I knew the

Ducharme family?" he said. They were the first words he had spoken since we'd sat down.

I nodded. He'd mentioned it right after Robbie was killed.

"We all did," he said.

We? All?

"Mr. Ducharme used to have a restaurant," he said. "Downtown, near police headquarters."

Cops, he meant. All the downtown cops knew the Ducharme family. All the homicide cops.

"They ran it together, Mr. and Mrs. Ducharme. Robbie used to hang around after school. This was when he was little. Mr. Ducharme closed the restaurant after his wife died. He owns a sandwich place now, near his house. The idea was, he could be right there for Robbie all the time."

I felt like telling him, no offense, but the last thing I'm interested in right now is Robbie and his family. If things had been different, maybe I would have come right out and said so.

"You know what happened to her?" Riel said. It was what Ms. Stephenson would call a rhetorical question, one where an answer isn't expected. How could I possibly know, except that Riel had just said she died?

"March break," Riel said. "When Robbie was ten. His mother took him to Disney World down in Florida. His father couldn't get away from work, so it was just the two of them." He reached for his beer and raised it to his lips before realizing that the bottle was empty.

"You want me to get you another one?" I said.

Riel shook his head. "So Robbie and his mother are down in Florida," he said. "And one night, instead of staying at Disney World, they decided to go exploring. Mr. Ducharme said his wife used to love to do that—get off the beaten path, you know."

I wondered why he was telling me about Robbie Ducharme's mother.

"While they were out exploring in Florida, Robbie's mother was mugged. It started out as a mugging, anyway. She'd sent Robbie into a store to get ice cream. She was waiting outside. And a guy with a gun comes up to her, tells her, give me your money. At least, that's what the police down there figure he must have said, because someone across the street saw her open her purse and take something out and hand it to the guy. The person across the street, he didn't see Mrs. Ducharme struggle or say anything to provoke the guy. But the guy shoots her anyway."

Jeez.

"That's when Robbie comes out of the store," Riel said. "So now the guy points his gun at Robbie." He looked down at the empty beer bottle again. "I bet Mr. Ducharme told the story a dozen times, like he just had to keep saying it, like he couldn't believe it." He looked back up at me. "Someone must have called the cops because all of a sudden they're there and they're yelling at the guy to drop his gun. But the guy doesn't. The cops have to shoot him. They find out later that he was seriously high. Too much stuff in his system, he's not thinking straight. And Robbie, he was just standing there. A little kid—ten years old. Up until then he hasn't said anything, hasn't cried. Nothing. Until the cops shoot the guy. Then he starts to cry." He got up, put his empty beer bottle back in the case, and poured himself a glass of water. He drank half of it before sitting down again. "The cop down there told me at first he thought maybe Robbie must have been hurt. Then he figured Robbie was in shock, like maybe he couldn't take in what had happened to his mother."

He looked across the table at me, as if he were waiting for me to say something. But what could you say after a story like that? All I could think of was what Robbie had said to me about Billy: *Who you cry over says everything.*

"Robbie was in therapy after that," Riel said. "I don't know if it explains everything about him, but, if you ask me, it explains a lot."

"I wish someone had told me," I said.

"Told you all about Robbie's life, you mean? Some kid you hardly knew, were never interested in?"

"Maybe I would have reacted differently."

"Sure," Riel said. "And maybe if somebody had told Robbie more about you, he wouldn't have said what he said. Only it doesn't work that way. Everybody has their own reasons for doing things—good or bad—and most of the time the rest of us don't know what they are. That's why it generally pays to give the other guy the benefit of the doubt."

Which I hadn't done in Robbie's case. I stared down at the half-eaten piece of pizza on my plate. I was still staring at it when I said, "So, what am I supposed to do now?"

"There's nothing you can do," Riel said. "Jonesy's a good cop. He knows how to keep an open mind until he has all the facts. He'll keep dogging it." He reached out, flipped the pizza box shut, then carried his plate to the sink and dropped what remained of his slice into the garbage.

"Am I grounded?" I said.

"Is that all you're going to eat?" Riel said.

I nodded. Riel took my plate. "No, you're not grounded," he said. "But it might be a good idea for you to stay put for a while."

I watched Riel clean up. It was hard to tell what he was really saying sometimes. I wasn't officially grounded, but I should probably stay put. Did that mean I *had* to stay in?

"I need to take a walk or something," I said. "You know, get some air."

Riel was wiping down the table with a damp cloth. He stopped what he was doing and peered hard at me. "If you go, you're going to come back, right?" he said.

The question threw me. "Yeah," I said. "Where else—" I saw some of the tension go out of Riel's body. He wasn't worried about what I might do when I went out. He was worried about whether I would come back. It made me feel a little better. "Yeah," I said. "I'm going to come back."

"You know your curfew, Mike," he said, more re-laxed now, sounding more like his regular self.

"Yeah."

» » »

I wondered if Riel would have let me leave the house if he'd known where I was planning to go. Probably not. So I was glad the subject hadn't come up. The last thing I wanted to do was lie to him again. He deserved better than that.

It was quiet on Jen's street. The sun had been down for at least half an hour. The streetlights had been on for longer than that. But it wasn't so late that people had pulled their curtains and drawn their drapes. As I walked down the sidewalk, I had a good view into most of the houses that lined the street. You could always see into houses early in the evening when it was dark outside and people had all their lights on inside. When I got to Jen's house I could see right into her living room and, beyond that, into the dining room. A man was standing between the two rooms—Jen's dad. He seemed to be talking to someone. Then I saw a willowy figure glide across the room in a long fluid movement. Jen. Moving like a bal-lerina. She wrapped her arms around her father's neck and went up on her tiptoes to kiss him on the cheek. Then Mr. Hayes disappeared from view. The porch light went on. I ducked behind the hedge that marked the front border of the property and peeked through it.

Mr. Hayes came out of the house and walked to the car that was parked in the driveway. I retreated a little further and crouched between the side of the hedge and a tree on a neighboring property until Mr. Hayes's BMW backed down the driveway and took off up the street.

After he had gone I crept back to the hedge and followed it, trying to keep myself out of the line of sight of the house. I tried to move as if I belonged in this neighborhood, so that the people who lived in the big houses wouldn't notice me, wouldn't peg me as an outsider, someone potentially up to no good. When I got to the edge of the driveway I slowed my pace. I looked down to where the garage was, behind the house but visible from the sidewalk, doing my best to make it seem that I just happened to be glancing in that direction. The Hayeses had his-and-hers Beemers. Both of the garage doors were open, so I could see that Mrs. Hayes's Beemer wasn't there, which meant that Mrs. Hayes wasn't home either. It had been a lousy day in a lousy week in what I sometimes thought of as a lousy life, but, finally, something was going right.

I turned back and walked up the flagstone path to the front porch. I drew in a deep breath and pressed the doorbell.

When Jen appeared at the door, I couldn't help it, my mouth dropped open. I hadn't been up close to her in nearly two months. I'd forgotten how beautiful she was, how creamy her skin was, how green her eyes were, how golden her hair was, how soft and pink her lips were.

When she pushed open the outer door, I inhaled the flowery scent of the perfume she always wore. I would have been in heaven, I might even have felt hope—if only she had been smiling.

Jen frowned at me. The hand holding open the outer door trembled. For a moment I was afraid she was going to step back into the house and shut me out. I wondered whether grabbing the door before she could close it would make things better or worse.

"You shouldn't be here," she said.

"I have to talk to you."

"The police were here. They asked me about where I was a couple of weeks ago—the night that kid was killed in the park."

When Jen was happy, when things were going her way, her green eyes were as cool and inviting as summer grass under a June sky. When she was mad, though, they were as hard and sharp and cold as emeralds. They were cold now.

"They came here and asked me all kinds of crazy questions," she said. "My dad almost had a heart attack he was so mad. What are you trying to do to me, Mike?"

Her hand moved again. She was going to go back inside. She was going to slam the door.

"I'm in big trouble, Jen," I said. "They think I was involved in what happened to Robbie."

A puzzled look played across her face. I tried to remember if she had ever been in any of Robbie's classes, but couldn't.

"Robbie Ducharme," I said. "The kid who was killed in the park."

And there it was. That cold look, the one that always reminded me of Jen's mother. And there was that tilt of her head as she crossed her arms over her chest and studied me again. Her expression, her whole body language, said, Yeah, that figures.

"You and your friends managed to get into *big* trouble this time, huh, Mike?"

I couldn't have felt worse if she'd kneed me.

"Jeez, Jen . . ."

She just stood with her arms crossed, her expression like winter, like she was the exterminator and I was the bug.

"If they asked you all those questions," I said, "then you've got to know where I told them I was." I wasn't sure how Detective Jones would have gone about it. Would he have said, *Michael McGill told us . . .* and then gone on to tell her the story I had told the cops? Or would he simply have asked her to account for her whereabouts that night and then maybe asked her questions about it? *So you're saying you weren't down on Eastern Avenue at around midnight, you're saying you didn't* meet *someone down there, you're saying you didn't* get *into a car?* Either way, Jen was smart. She had to have figured it out.

Maybe if I hadn't been working so hard to convince her to help me, and maybe if BMWs weren't so well made and didn't run so quietly, I would have noticed that Mr. Hayes had returned. Maybe if Mr. Hayes had closed his car door when he got out or maybe if he'd turned off the engine, I would have noticed that he was coming up the flagstone path behind me. But Mr. Hayes didn't do any of those things, so I didn't notice, not until a hand grabbed me by the upper arm and spun me around, not until I was actually staring into Mr. Hayes's furious face.

"Jennifer, go back inside," he said. His hand was as tight and hard as a vise grip. There were going to be bruises, for sure. "And *you*—" If he'd yanked any harder on my arm, he would have dislocated it. "You get out of here before I call the police."

"Daddy—" Jen said.

"I said, go inside," he yelled at her. With each word his fingers bit a little deeper into my arm. Mr. Hayes had a grip like iron. I knew he belonged to a gym. He worked out four or five times a week. Played racquetball. Went mountain biking with a couple of lawyers the same age as him, looking for that forever-young experience. I used to think it was pretty funny, guys pushing fifty acting like they were closer to fifteen. I had never considered that all that working out could make Mr. Hayes a truly scary guy, a guy who, if he didn't hang on to that temper of his, could do some serious damage. I thought about it now, though.

Jen retreated into the house and closed the outer door, but she left the heavy inside door open and stood her ground behind it, watching through the glass.

"You," Mr. Hayes said, pressing his face in close to mine, "you stay off my property and away from my daughter. You got that?"

I nodded. No way was I going to argue with this guy.

Mr. Hayes released me with a shove that sent me careening backward down the porch steps. I had to grab the railing to keep from falling. Mr. Hayes started down the steps toward me, his eyes on fire. He couldn't have been scarier if he'd been a hundred-pound Rottweiler with a law degree. I scrambled backward down the rest of the steps, then turned and retreated down the path to the sidewalk. Mr. Hayes came down a few steps. I drew back even farther and crossed the street. Only then did he turn. Only then did he guide Jen back into the house, away from the door. Then he came out again, down the path to his car. He pulled a jug of milk from the front seat before closing and locking the car. Well, that figured, The guy pays who-knew-how-much to belong to a gym, but when he needs a jug of milk, what does he do? He jumps in his Beemer and drives all of three blocks to the closest 7–Eleven.

CHAPTER NINE

Whenever I had a bad day—when I got in trouble with a teacher or when Vin was acting like a jerk for some reason, or when I'd had my heart set on something that I ended up not getting, like being tagged to play forward in soccer when I was nine—my mom used to say, "Tomorrow is another day." She said it as if it were a good thing, as if I should look forward to the next day because, as she said, "You never know what it's going to bring."

Except that sometimes you did know. And sometimes what it was bringing was something no one in his right mind would look forward to.

Like meeting with Rhona Katz. It wasn't Rhona so much. She was okay. Pretty. And I bet she was a real tiger in court. But it was the fact of having to meet with her. Being in that much trouble that all of a sudden I was a guy who needed a lawyer.

Riel put on a jacket and tie to take me down to her office, which I couldn't figure out. Rhona was supposed to be an old friend of his. Who was he trying to impress? Or maybe I had been wrong about him and Susan. Maybe they really were just good friends.

At the meeting, Rhona—Riel made me call her *Ms. Katz*—wanted the same thing as the cops. She wanted all the so-called facts of the case.

"Tell me everything," she said. "And I do mean everything. Every detail you can remember. Anyone you noticed on the street. Anyone who might have noticed you, even if you don't know their names."

I told her the whole story—again—stopping whenever she raised her hand. She was writing everything down, and sometimes I talked too fast for her. I wanted never to have to tell it again. I wanted it to end. She wanted what she called "a complete record."

After I told it again, I answered all of her questions. Then I said, "I didn't do anything."

Rhona just nodded. She looked at Riel as she said, "He was seen fighting with Robbie." I bristled at that. I hadn't been fighting with Robbie. I had shoved him. Once. That was all. "He was seen near the park the night it happened. He has an alibi that doesn't seem to be holding water at the moment. They may try to get a search warrant—they may want to see if they can find the clothes he was wearing that night, check for blood. You know the drill, John."

I couldn't begin to remember what I had been wearing

two whole weeks ago. Anyway, whatever it was, it had probably been through the laundry by now.

"I'm going to contact the girl," Rhona said. She consulted a file. "Jennifer Hayes. See if I can talk to her. Also Ashley Tierney and her mother."

Riel nodded. Meeting adjourned.

We got to school in time for second period. I got to my English class just as the bell rang. I tried to catch Sal's eye as I made my way to my seat, but he was staring down at his desk and didn't look up. When class finished he bolted from the room. I tried to follow him, but Ms. Stephenson called my name and crooked a finger to get me to go to her desk.

"Your essay on Hamlet," she said.

"What essay on Hamlet?"

"Exactly," Ms. Stephenson said. "It was due on Friday, Mike."

I had completely forgotten.

"Get it in tomorrow and I'll only take ten points off. Any later than that, and you start losing five points a day. Got it, Mike?"

If things are going to go bad, why not go all the way? I sighed and nodded.

By the time I got out of Ms. Stephenson's classroom, Sal had been swallowed up among the thirteen hundred kids who were on lunch—assuming he was still on school property and hadn't taken off to one of the zillion restaurants along Gerrard Street or hadn't gone over to Gerrard Square. It was obvious he was trying to avoid me. Maybe he felt bad about talking to the police. For sure I would have felt bad if I'd been in the same situation—especially if I had told the police something that would make Sal look bad, which I was pretty sure I would never do. But how was Sal supposed to have known? I had never told him that I'd lied to Riel about how I got my hands all banged up. And who knows how the cops asked him the question? The poor guy probably didn't have a clue what they were after. And that's what I wanted to tell him—it's not your fault.

Cat, though, Cat was something else. Cat knew exactly what she was doing when she talked to the cops. They didn't even have to ask her. She had *volunteered* the information. *Wrong information*. If I ran into Cat . . . Jeez, I had no idea what I'd do if I ran into Cat.

"Hey, Mike." Vin caught me by the arm.

I shook free, mad at him too. Vin, who adored Cat. Sweet little Cat. Yeah, right. I turned, headed for the nearest exit and pushed my way out into the schoolyard.

"Hey, Mikey, wait up!" Vin burst out the door behind me. "Hey!" He caught me by the arm again and this time when I tried to shake him off, he held tight. "What's the matter with you?"

My hands clenched into fists as I faced my old friend. Old as in *used-to-be*.

"What?" I said. "She didn't tell you?"

"Who?"

"*Who?*" Like there were so many *shes* in Vin's life.

"You mean Cat?"

I just stared at him.

"Tell me what?" Vin said. He looked genuinely baffled.

I studied his face. We had been friends since we were five years old. We'd both been in and out of a lot of trouble since then. We'd had our differences too. And over that time I had learned a few things about Vin. One, Vin could sling the bull with the best of them. He'd got me going more than once about things that turned out to be his idea of a joke. Two, when he was slinging away, and when it was a good story he was slinging, he eventually gave himself away. Usually it was his eyes that did it. They just couldn't stay focused on his victim the whole time. They always shifted away. Most people didn't realize that, but I had caught onto it and, after that, Vin had never been able to put one over on me.

So I peered at him now to see whether his eyes would shift.

They didn't.

He stared right back at me, two little lines between his eyes, shaking his head slightly.

"Come on, Mike," he said. "What's going on?" He really seemed to have no idea.

I unclenched my fists and let out a long sigh. I looked out across the schoolyard. There were kids everywhere, talking, laughing, smoking, flirting, shooting hoops. Probably some of them were complaining too. Some of them were thinking, *Boy, this is not my day.* Thinking, *I have problems.* Probably even thinking they had *big* problems. Did they ever have it wrong!

"The cops asked me more questions," I said.

Vin shook his head again. "What about?" he said, like he couldn't figure it out.

"About the Robbie Ducharme thing."

"What? Are they crazy? They think you had something to do with that?"

"Yeah," I said. "They do."

"I don't get it. Why would they think that?"

I studied him again. And again Vin's eyes held firm on my own.

"Because of Cat," I said.

"Cat?" Vin reacted as if I had said Hamlet told them I'd been involved. Or better, The ghost of Hamlet's father appeared to the cops and told them. "*My* Cat, you mean?"

I nodded. "She told the cops she saw me fighting with Robbie Ducharme."

This seemed to be news to Vin. "You were in a fight with Robbie Ducharme?"

"He said something to me once. About Billy. I shoved him and he fell and whacked his head. Cat saw."

Vin seemed to relax a little. "So the cops were probably asking around about you and Robbie and she just told them what she saw." He seemed relieved, as if what she had done was okay with him.

"She also told them she saw me fighting with him the day before he died," I said.

"Jeez, you really had it in for the guy," Vin said. He looked at me with new interest. "What did he say to you anyway?"

"She lied," I said.

"What?"

"Cat. She lied to the cops when she said she saw me fighting with Robbie before he died. I don't even remember seeing him that day."

Vin didn't say anything. He stared down at the ground, shaking his head, like he was having a hard time digesting this last piece of information.

"Your *girlfriend* lied about me to the cops, Vin," I said. "And because of that I'm in big trouble. Riel had to get me a lawyer. And the lawyer says the cops are probably going to get a search warrant to see if they can tie me to being in the park or to Robbie." I shuddered when I remembered how Rhona had put it. *Check for blood*, she had said.

"Jeez," Vin said. It came out like a long, sad breath. "I don't get it. Why would Cat do something like that?" Then, before I could even ask—and I wasn't sure that I had been going to ask—Vin said, "I'll talk to her. If she lied—"

If?

"She lied, Vin."

"I'll talk to her, Mike. I promise."

» » »

Oh boy, math. Just the thing to take a guy's mind off the fact that the cops think he's been involved in stomping someone to death. The perfect way to distract a guy from the fact that his used-to-be-best friend's girlfriend lied about him to the cops. The cure-all that would let a guy forget for a little while that the cops believed *her* and didn't believe *him* because he's already been caught in half a dozen lies. Stupid lies. Things that, now that I thought about it, I shouldn't have lied about. Note to self for the future: If you decide, for whatever dumb reason, that you've got to lie about something, make it something big, something important, something life-and-death. And, oh yeah, have a larger-than-life reason for it so that if you get caught—knowing my luck, *when* you get caught—at least you can console yourself with the fact that you lied for a *very* good reason.

Of course, math didn't take my mind off anything, didn't distract me, wasn't a cure-all. It just embarrassed me because Mr. Tran sent me up to the board to write out a problem that he had assigned for homework. A problem that I had attempted to solve. I really had, it's the truth. But math and I weren't exactly on the same wavelength. I got the problem hopelessly wrong, which exasperated Mr. Tran. Mr. Tran, unlike Riel, is the kind of teacher who thinks that lack of results is due to lack of effort. If you get it wrong, it's because you didn't try. So naturally he assigned me ten more problems for homework. To help me, you know? So that I'd have to try.

"Do *all* of them, Mike," he said. "I expect to see them in my box first thing tomorrow morning."

Yes, sir.

After math, I discovered that I had left my history assignment in my locker. At least, I hoped that was where I had left it, because if it wasn't there, then it was at home. And if it was at home, I was going to get into trouble with yet another teacher. Could the day get any better?

I spun the combination on my lock and opened my locker. The top shelf was a clutter of textbooks, notebooks, old assignments and test papers, some of which had overflowed onto the floor of my locker. I began to root through the pile on top. Not there.

I slammed my fist into the open locker door.

The thing was, I had *done* the stupid assignment. Unlike my English essay, which, I admit, I had forgotten, I had actually done my history homework. But if I couldn't find it, if I showed up without it and said, "I lost it," or "I must have left it at home," there was no way Mr. Danos was going to believe me. I'd be in trouble again. And there would be one more example of Michael McGill not telling it like it is, spinning it out, trying to get by on yet another lie.

Terrific.

I looked down at the overflow on the floor of my locker. It was theoretically possible that my assignment had slipped down there. Why not? After all, it was also theoretically possible that I could travel back to the time

CHAPTER EIGHT

I heard Riel suck in a lungful of air. I wished I could do the same, but my throat had closed up. At least, that's what it felt like. I couldn't breathe. Except for little flashes of light popping on and off like fireflies on a summer night, the room went dark around me. I felt a hand on my arm. Rhona Katz's hand, not Riel's hand.

"Mike, are you okay?" she said. My lawyer asking me, not Riel.

Then someone pressed a paper cup into my hand and guided the cup to my mouth. Water. The room lightened up a little, and I almost started to cry. Riel was on his feet beside me, pushing me to drink the water. I choked it down. After he checked to make sure that I had drunk it all, he crumpled the paper cup and tossed it into a wastepaper basket in the corner. He dropped a hand onto my shoulder, just for a second, and then he sat down beside me again.

Somebody saw you with him, Mike.

"What do you mean?" I said. "Who saw me?" But that wasn't the right question. The right question was, How could someone have possibly seen me?

"Suppose you tell us," Detective London said. I smelled his onion breath again and it made my stomach churn.

"I didn't see Robbie a week ago Monday," I said. I was sure of it. Well, pretty sure.

Detective Jones watched me closely. "You're hesitating, Mike," he said.

I reran the past two weeks in my head. When you watch cop shows on TV, the cop says, *Mr. Brown, can you account for your movements on the night of January eighteenth?* It doesn't matter if January eighteenth was weeks ago or months ago, Mr. Brown thinks for a couple of seconds and then he says, *Certainly officer. I was at the opera with my mother-in-law.* Well, Mr. Brown and all those other TV suspects must have been popping the gingko pills because they had much better memories than me. Or maybe their lives were more interesting. Maybe, for them, every day wasn't exactly the same as every other day, they didn't all blend together so you could barely remember what day of the week it was, let alone which of thirteen hundred faces you saw at school on one particular day versus another particular day.

"I don't know," I said. If they asked me to swear on the Bible, that's what I'd have to say. *I don't know.* "Maybe I passed him in the hall or something."

of the dinosaurs. Still . . .

I crouched down to begin looking.

And then I found myself in one of those moments.

They happen sometimes, those moments that last about a split second, when three or four or five things—*big* things—happen all at once. Those moments that, when you look back at them later, you can see each thing separately, like a little movie. You can see each one unfold, and then you can see the exact moment where they all collide, changing your life forever.

I crouched down to look into the jumble of papers and spotted a bag that looked suspiciously like a lunch bag—a lunch bag that didn't look empty, which meant there was a sandwich in there somewhere, one that I didn't remember, which meant that it had been there for a while. Well, there was no way I was going to deal with that right now. I was down there on my haunches, thinking about my history assignment, thinking about how old the lunch in that bag might be, when I also started thinking about the time—specifically, how much of it I had left before I would be late for history class. I turned to look at the clock halfway down the hall. And time splintered.

As I turned my head, I glimpsed something gleaming in the bottom of my locker. My brain processed what I saw in that fraction of a second: a watch.

My head continued to turn and my eyes began to zero in on the clock on the wall. But they ended up focusing on something else instead—on Ms. Rather, the school principal, standing at the end of the hall, talking to two men. Two men in uniforms. Two cops.

My eyes continued their sweep upward until they saw the clock. Three minutes. I had three minutes until the bell rang and I'd be officially late for history.

My head started to turn back toward my locker so that I could continue to search for my history assignment. On the way, I looked at Ms. Rather again. Then I looked at my locker. But instead of continuing my search for my history assignment, I reached out for the thing that had glinted at me from the bottom of my locker. The watch. But it wasn't *my* watch. My watch was, well, I wasn't 100 percent sure where it was. At Riel's somewhere. In my room somewhere. So whose watch was this?

I picked it up. I looked at it. Then I realized that picking it up had probably not been such a great idea.

It was a nice watch.

A good watch.

An expensive watch. Solid, not like the one I owned.

And this watch was engraved.

To Robert.

From Grandpa.

Robert.

Robbie.

I stole a glance down the hall.

Cops. Standing there with Ms. Rather.

They'll probably try to get a search warrant . . .

Robbie Ducharme's watch.

In *my* locker.

When I thought about it later, it seemed to me that my movements were slow and heavy, as if someone had hit the slo-mo button on my life.

I slipped the watch into my pocket. Then, without looking down the hall to where the cops were, I stood up, closed my locker, locked it and slipped into the closest stairwell. I went down the stairs two at a time. The bell rang when I was halfway down. It didn't matter anymore. I didn't care. Instead of reporting to Mr. Danos's history class, I kept going down the stairs until I reached the main floor. From there I pushed out the exit, which opened onto the east side of the school. I saw a cop car parked in front of the school. Another car pulled up right behind it. It wasn't splashed all over with Toronto Police Service decals and it didn't have a cherry on top, but I knew it was a cop car all the same. Detectives Jones and London got out and headed for the main entrance to the school. I hung back until they had gone inside. Then I ran for the streetcar that was stopped at the red light on Gerrard.

The front door of the streetcar was open. I ducked in, fishing in my pocket for my student card and a couple of mangled transit tickets I was sure were somewhere at the bottom of one of my pockets.

Someone yelled something when I bounded up the steps to drop my ticket into the box. I didn't catch the words. They were in Spanish. But I did catch the expression on the driver's face. It was the same expression you'd expect to see on the face of a man who was being held up at gunpoint. He gestured at me with his head—nodding toward the door. Then someone yelled something in Spanish again. I turned and smiled when I recognized Sal's dad.

"Hi," I said. Or maybe I just started to say it. I'm not entirely sure. Because while I was saying hi—or while I was starting to say hi—I realized that something was wrong. At first I thought it was the fact that Sal's dad was standing in the aisle instead of sitting down. There were plenty of empty seats. Then I thought, *No, that isn't it.* It was the way the other passengers were looking at him. There were maybe ten or a dozen passengers in all, most of them women. Two men, both of them old. Retired people, I figured. People who could be on the streetcar at two in the afternoon because they didn't have to be at a job or at school. All of the passengers were staring at Sal's dad. Or, I realized slowly, not at Sal's dad, but at his hand. Actually, at what he was holding in his hand—a hammer. What was Sal's dad doing on the streetcar with a hammer?

Sal's dad yelled something else in Spanish. He raised the hammer when he shouted and seemed to be shaking it at a woman who was sitting close by. The woman ducked down in her seat. I heard a sound like crying. Jeez, what was going on?

"Close it, close it, close it, close it, close it, close it, close it," Sal's dad shouted over and over again. He shook the hammer at another woman. She screamed and then started to cry.

"Close the door," she yelled at the streetcar driver. "He wants you to close the door."

The driver reached for the controls and shut the front door to the streetcar. Then he collapsed in his seat.

"Now what?" he said. He spoke softly. It took me a moment to realize that he was asking Sal's dad.

"Mr. San Miguel, are you okay?" I said.

At the sound of his name, Sal's dad zeroed in on me. He shook the hammer at me. I retreated a step—a reflex action. The woman who had ducked down in her seat peeked up. Tears were streaming down her face.

"You know this guy?" the streetcar driver asked me in a voice that wasn't much louder than a whisper.

I nodded.

"Is he on drugs or something?" the driver said in an even quieter voice, as if he were afraid of what might happen if Sal's dad heard the question. "First he wants everything open. Now he wants everything closed."

I took another look at Sal's dad and shook my head. Then, out of the corner of my eye, I caught the flash of lights. From where I was standing I saw one, two, three, jeez, four cop cars pull up—one in front of the streetcar, blocking it from moving forward, another right behind it, and one on each side. Then another cop car pulled up, and another. No wonder Sal's dad wanted the doors closed now. After what had happened at his house, he was probably afraid.

All the cops stood well away from the streetcar,

behind their cars. A bunch of them huddled together. They were trying to figure out exactly what was going on, I guess, so that they could decide what to do about it. I looked back over my shoulder at the streetcar driver, who was smiling cautiously now. He must have called it in, and the transit authorities must have called the cops.

"Hello in the streetcar," a voice boomed over a loudspeaker. I looked out of the window and saw a plainclothes police officer standing behind one of the squad cars. I also saw that it was getting darker outside, even though it was early in the afternoon. Big black clouds had rolled in.

"Hello in the streetcar," the voice boomed again. "This is Sergeant O'Connell. I'm going to ask the driver to open the doors to the car so that all the passengers can come out."

The woman who had been crying started to wipe at her tears. Other passengers looked over to whichever door was closer to them, the front or the back. The streetcar driver started to reach for the controls, but Sal's dad shook his head—and he kept shaking it, back and forth, back and forth, tick-tock, tick-tock—as he shouted, "Keep closed, keep closed, keep closed!"

The driver looked at Sal's dad, who was halfway down the car. Then he looked out into the street where there were a half dozen police cars and twice as many cops, all with guns. *He's going to open the doors*, I thought. Then, as if I'd been hit by a hurricane or a tidal wave, I was flung to one side and was toppling toward an empty seat. But instead of landing safely on the upholstery, I struck the metal bar that ran up alongside the seat. It caught me in the ribs, knocking the air out of me and sending pain searing up my left side.

Sal's dad had pushed me aside as he rushed up to the driver, swinging his hammer. He was a lot shorter than me; his head barely cleared my shoulder. But, man, was he strong!

The driver let out a shout, and for one horrible moment I thought that maybe Sal's dad had hit him with the hammer. But, as far as I could tell, he hadn't. As far as I could tell, he had shoved the driver, just like he had shoved me. Now he was standing over the driver, shaking his hammer at him and saying something in Spanish.

"Juan," a voice—Sergeant O'Connell's voice—was saying. "Juan San Miguel, do you hear me?"

At the mention of his name, Sal's dad half-turned. One of his hands gripped the streetcar driver's arm. The other gripped the hammer. He pulled the driver up out of his seat and pushed him down the aisle toward the rest of the passengers.

I glanced out the window of the streetcar. A crowd had gathered now—people from the neighborhood, people from school, Sal. I spotted Sal making his way through the crowd toward the police, trying to get to Sergeant O'Connell. He must have heard his father's name over the loudspeaker. A cop tried to hold him back, but Sal started talking fast. Whatever he was saying got the cop's attention. The cop led him through to where Sergeant O'Connell was standing. Sal started talking to the sergeant, straining toward him as if that would help to make his point. Then Sergeant O'Connell was talking to Sal and Sal was nodding. I'd never seen Sal look more serious. He was staring up at the big police officer. His attention seemed to be 100 percent focused on whatever the sergeant was saying to him. Sergeant O'Connell handed him the microphone.

Sal started talking. In Spanish.

Sal's dad turned toward the window.

The driver started to get up from the seat where he was sitting, but one of the women—not one of the ones who had been crying, but another one—laid a hand on his arm. She didn't say a word. She just shook her head and then nodded toward the window. The driver settled back into his seat.

Sal kept talking, fast, in Spanish. I didn't understand a single word he said. Sal's dad seemed to be listening, but he was still gripping the hammer and holding it high. From the tone of his voice, I guessed that Sal was pleading with his father—*Let the driver open the doors, let the passengers get out.*

Sal's dad stood where he was.

I saw Sergeant O'Connell take the microphone back from Sal.

"Mr. San Miguel," he said. "Juan. Whatever the problem is, I'm sure we can work it out."

He held the microphone out to Sal, who spoke again in Spanish. Translating, I guessed. I glanced at the driver and wondered what he had told the transit authorities. I wondered if he'd said that Sal's dad had a hammer or if he'd just said that he was armed. When I glanced back out the window, I saw that it had started to rain. I also saw that Sergeant O'Connell wasn't holding the microphone up anymore. Instead, he was talking to a couple of other cops. Sal was shaking his head. He looked upset. Something was happening—or was about to happen. Something bad.

"Mr. San Miguel," I said. I kept my voice low, spoke softly so that I wouldn't startle him or upset him. "Hey, Mr. San Miguel, remember me?" I don't know how he wouldn't remember me—I stopped by Sal's house almost every day. Sal and I had been hanging out together for a couple of years now. But I didn't know much about what was wrong with Sal's dad. "It's me," I said. "Mike. Sal's friend. Remember?"

Sal's dad looked at me like I was some new species of Martian who had just landed.

"Mr. San Miguel," I said, "I see Sal out there. Do you see him?" Sal's dad was staring at me. "He's right out there," I said, pointing to where Sal was standing. "See him? He's right there, and he needs to talk to you. He looks like whatever he wants to tell you is pretty important. Maybe you should let him come inside, Mr. San Miguel," I said. "What do you say?"

Sal's dad looked out the window. So did I. More

cops had joined the huddle. They looked deadly serious. They weren't going to rush the streetcar, were they? They couldn't possibly be planning to shoot—could they? The cops had been called twice to Sal's house in the past couple of weeks. Both times it was because Sal's dad had been threatening someone—first with a weed whacker, then with hedge clippers. Just ordinary stuff that most people had around the house, like most people had hammers. Ordinary stuff that could be used as weapons. And when they were used as weapons, the cops got upset. They'd arrested Sal's dad when he refused to put down the hedge clippers. What would they do to him now that he was holding people hostage on a streetcar, threatening them with a hammer?

I started down the aisle toward Sal's dad. My side felt like it was on fire.

"Hey, Mr. San Miguel," I said. I smiled at him. "Sal's out there and he needs to talk to you real bad. Maybe he's hurt. Maybe something's wrong with Sal, Mr. San Miguel. Don't you think we should find out?"

The hand holding the hammer relaxed a little as Sal's dad peered out the window, looking for Sal.

I held my breath and said a little prayer as I reached out and grabbed the hammer from his hand. This time when the driver tried to get up out of his seat, no one tried to stop him. He grabbed Sal's dad from behind and held him tight. Sal's dad struggled.

"The door," the driver said. He told me how to open it. I ran back up the aisle, still carrying the hammer, and followed the driver's instructions. And then there were cops everywhere.

It was pouring outside now. The crowd had retreated. All the people who were left—and I was surprised how many there were—were jammed together under store awnings or in bus shelters or under the overhang of the school.

Cops surrounded Sal's dad and put handcuffs on him. Other cops checked to see if the passengers were okay and took down their names, addresses and phone numbers. Then the passengers were allowed to leave. One of them, an old man, didn't want to get off. He had to get home, he kept telling the cop who was trying to get him to leave. The cop had to promise that someone would drive him home. The cops talked to me too. The driver kept telling them how I had talked to the crazy man, how I had taken the hammer away from him.

"He's not crazy," I said. "He's just sick, that's all."

I looked outside and saw Sal standing in the rain. Finally the cops let me leave. I stepped down out of the streetcar and into the rain, scanning the crowd. I saw Vin and Cat, huddled together near the school. I saw Rebecca with the red hair. I saw A. J. and his friends. And coming toward me, I saw Riel, his face a mixture of astonishment and worry and relief.

"You okay?" he said when he reached me. He didn't seem to notice that he was getting drenched. We both were.

"You kidding?" said a voice behind me. The driver's voice. "He took the weapon away from the guy."

Riel looked at me more closely now. "You okay?" he said again.

I nodded. As Riel led me back toward the school, I felt the watch in my pocket. Robbie Ducharme's watch.

CHAPTER TEN

The cops wanted to talk to me. Reporters had shown up and found out what I had done, and they wanted to talk to me too. People on the street and kids from school had found out, and they all pressed in close around me, which is scarier than you'd think. Crowds had never bothered me before, but now I found myself thinking about what would happen to me if everyone came at me at the same time from all directions.

Riel put a hand on my shoulder and led me through the crowd into the school and then into the staff lounge. Ms. Rather was standing at the door. Riel went over to speak with her. The next thing I knew, she was clearing everyone out of the room.

The teachers all had lockers. Riel went to his, opened it, and pulled out a T-shirt and a sweatshirt. He tossed the sweatshirt to me.

"You're wet," he said. "Go dry off and put this on. As

soon as you talk to the police, I'll take you home."

I went into one of the bathrooms and pulled off my wet shirt. I dried my skin and my hair as best as I could with paper towel, then pulled on Riel's sweatshirt. When I opened the bathroom door to go back out, I saw Riel getting ready to pull on the T-shirt. I stared at him. I realized I'd never seen him without a shirt on, but that wasn't why I was staring. I was staring because of the scar on Riel's chest. It was big and ragged and angry-looking. Billy had told me that Riel had been shot and his partner had been killed. That's why he wasn't a cop anymore. But Billy had never said where Riel had been shot. Maybe he didn't know. And Riel never said anything about it.

Riel looked at me looking at his scar, then he pulled the T-shirt down over it. He went to the door of the teachers' lounge and let two cops in. One of them was Sergeant O'Connell.

"Hello, Mike," he said. He smiled. His tone was friendly. It was the first time in a long time that a cop had been friendly to me. "Are you okay?"

I nodded. "How's Mr. San Miguel?" I asked.

"He's not hurt," the sergeant said. "But he's ill. We've taken him to the hospital to make sure he gets looked after."

I wondered how Sal was and whether anyone had told Mrs. San Miguel yet.

"That was very brave, what you did," the sergeant said. "In a situation like that, there's always the risk that someone could get hurt."

"Mr. San Miguel wouldn't hurt anyone," I said. "He was a professor back home in Guatemala. He taught poetry."

This seemed to surprise Sergeant O'Connell. "It would be helpful, Mike," he said, "if you can tell me everything you can remember about what happened after you got on the streetcar. Think you could do that?"

"Helpful to who?" I asked. Riel frowned at the question, but he didn't say anything. "I'll tell you anyway," I said to Sergeant O'Connell. "I'm just wondering, that's all." Would anything I said hurt Sal's dad?

"That's okay," Sergeant O'Connell said. "Nobody was hurt, and that's good. It would be helpful to everyone, including Mr. San Miguel, if we know exactly what happened. You know he needs help, right, Mike?"

Yeah, I knew. I sat down on one of the sofas in the lounge and told Sergeant O'Connell everything I could remember. The cop with him wrote down everything I said.

"Is that it?" Riel said when I had finished.

Sergeant O'Connell nodded.

By then I was shivering. I had on Riel's dry sweatshirt, but my pants had got wet and they were making me cold.

"Come on, Mike," Riel said. He led me out of the room, through the rush of reporters and TV cameras, and down to the staff parking area. The reporters followed, but Riel kept a hand on my shoulder and wouldn't let them get to me. He helped me get into the car and then he got in himself. The reporters crowded around, but that didn't stop Riel. He inched the car forward.

As soon as I got home I knew that something was wrong in my room. It wasn't messy—well, it wasn't any messier than usual—but I could tell that someone had been in it.

"They were here with a warrant," Riel said. "Rhona was with them."

Oh.

"They searched your locker at school too," Riel said. Then he added, "How come you were on that streetcar at two o'clock in the afternoon, Mike? You were supposed to be in history class."

I had promised myself that I wouldn't lie to Riel anymore. And I had meant it—at the time.

"I just couldn't take it," I said. "All those questions from the cops. People thinking I did something when I didn't." I made myself look directly into Riel's eyes. "Sometimes I hate being at that school, you know? Everybody there thinks I'm screwed up, that I'm some kind of hopeless case, you know?"

"You can't control what people think, Mike," Riel said. "You can only lead your life right. Put on some dry clothes. I'm going to take a shower."

When I was alone in my room, I took off my wet clothes and pulled on some dry jeans and one of my own sweatshirts. Before I put my wet things in the hamper in my bathroom, I pulled the watch out of my pocket and looked at it again. Robbie's watch. It had been in my locker. I glanced around the room. In the end, I stashed the watch in the toe of an old sneaker in my closet. The cops had already searched the place. I didn't think there was much chance they'd search it again.

» » »

I called Sal's house maybe twenty, twenty-five times that night. Each time, the line was busy. Sal's family had an answering machine, but they didn't have call answer.

"Think I could go over there?" I asked Riel after supper.

"I think you should stay here and do your homework," Riel said.

"Yeah, but Sal—"

"Sal's probably got enough to think about for one day. Let him focus on his mom and dad. Maybe you could leave a little early tomorrow for school, stop by his house."

I said sure, because I had enough to think about too.

» » »

Sal was sitting on the front steps when I got there. He stood up when he saw me and came down the walk toward me.

"How's your dad?" I asked.

"He's in the hospital," Sal said. He looked terrible.

His face was pale, and he had dark circles under his eyes. His hair was standing up in a hundred different directions. "Psych ward."

"Did they arrest him?"

Sal shook his head no. "But he's not allowed to leave the hospital until the doctors say he can." He glanced back toward the house. "My mom was crying all night." Sal's lip trembled, and for a moment I thought he was going to start to cry too, which would have been okay with me. "Hey, Mike?"

I waited.

"What you did? Thanks. I was afraid the cops were going to storm the streetcar or something. I was afraid they were going to shoot him."

"I knew your dad would never hurt anyone, Sal," I said.

And then, jeez, there it was. Sal was crying. Not blubbering, but he was definitely leaking tears and wiping them away with the back of his hand. I didn't say anything about that. Instead I said, "You going to school today?"

He shook his head.

"Want me to bring your homework?"

Sal nodded, but I knew from the spaced-out look in his eyes that he was nodding by reflex, not because he actually cared.

"I'll come by later, okay?" I said.

He nodded again.

» » »

I noticed the red hair—how could I not notice it burning like fire in the morning sun?—before I registered that it was *her* hair. Rebecca was standing on a corner a couple of blocks from school. She kept looking around, as if she was waiting for someone. Then her eyes locked onto me. Well, that was that. Now she was going to turn and flee in the opposite direction for sure. I didn't understand why she reacted to me the way she did, but I didn't have to be pulling straight As to figure out that she didn't like me.

So I was surprised when she walked straight toward me, looking at me the whole time, like *I* was the person she had been waiting for. Or maybe someone was coming up behind me and Rebecca was walking toward *that* person. I glanced over my shoulder. There was no one behind me. When I turned back, she had stopped in front of me.

"Hi," she said. She was looking me over. She peered deep into my eyes again. I noticed that her eyes were dark brown, with little sparkles of gold in them.

"Hi," I said.

I glanced around, looking for that hidden camera or that group of girls who had dared her—*Betcha don't have the nerve to go and talk to the bad boy.* I didn't see anything out of the ordinary—well, besides Rebecca standing right there in front of me, staring into my eyes.

"I heard what you did on that streetcar," she said. "With that man who was sick."

The man who was sick. She hadn't said *the crazy man* or

the violent man or the man with the hammer. She had said that man who was sick. She'd said it as if she understood what had happened. It made me look at her with new interest.

"I thought about it all night," she said.

I was doing a little thinking of my own. *Why is she talking to me?*

"I don't get it," she said.

Get what?

"It was a good thing to do," she said. "Not everybody would have done that."

"I didn't want anyone to get hurt," I said.

"That's what I don't get."

I started to get a bad feeling about where this was going.

"So I don't get how you could help that man the way you did," she said, "and also be involved in what happened in the park."

"*What?*"

"I saw," she said.

I felt myself go cold all over. The bright sunny morning turned chilly and dark.

Jeez, I thought—*her, too?*

» » »

I knew Vin's schedule cold, so it was no big deal to scoot from music to Vin's computer class, which was two classrooms down, and grab Vin just as he was coming out the door. He looked surprised to see me.

"I gotta talk to you," I said.

"Yeah, sure," Vin said. "We'll hook up at lunch."

"I gotta talk to you *now*." I nodded toward the stairwell. "Come on."

"What about class?"

"This is important, Vin. Way more important than whatever lame class you have next."

"Yeah?" Vin said. "Even if it's Cop Boy's class? In fact—" He gave his head a little nod, and I saw Riel down the hall, talking to another teacher. Riel saw me too.

I grabbed Vin by the arm and dragged him toward the stairwell. I led him down to the ground floor and out behind the school.

"Jeez," Vin said, "this better be important. Riel knows I'm here, so if I ditch his class he's going make me write an extra essay or something."

"You have to tell them, Vin."

"What?" Vin looked confused. I could imagine the questions popping into his head. *Tell who? Tell them what?*

"You have to tell the cops exactly what happened in the park the night Robbie Ducharme died," I said.

Vin stared at me. Then he laughed. "This is a joke, right?" he said. "You're jazzing me, right, Mike? Last I heard, some guy said he'd seen you near the park that night." He seemed to think that was funny. "And the cops were here with a search warrant yesterday. They were going through your locker." He stopped and looked at me. "Everything's okay, isn't it, Mike?"

"What do you mean?"

There, his eyes shifted away from mine. Now I knew for sure something was wrong.

"Did they find anything?" he asked.

"There was nothing to find," I said.

I saw a flicker of something—what? relief?—on his face.

"I don't get it," I said. "We were friends. Best friends. At least, I thought we were."

"We *are* friends," Vin said. His smile was a little shaky. "What's the matter with you, Mike?"

"I found something in my locker," I said. "And you're the only person who could have put it there."

Now Vin really did laugh. Except it was a kind of nervous laugh. "Yeah, right," he said. "There's only about a hundred people who know how to get into your locker."

"I changed the combination," I said. "Remember?"

"Yeah. And right away you told me the new one. I bet you told Sal and—"

"You know Riel," I said. "You know what he's like. My math book disappeared from my locker right after I started living with him, and he went ballistic. I must have heard ten different lectures—*long* lectures—about how he expects me to be responsible, keep track of my stuff, how if anything gets lost, I have to pay for it. So I got a new lock and I promised I wouldn't tell anyone else the combination."

"Yeah, but you did. You told me."

"You're the only person I told," I said. "And I only

told you because you were desperate to get your hands on my French book because you'd left yours at home. And because you were my best friend."

Vin's smile vanished. "Are you saying you think *I* put Robbie's watch in your locker?"

I shook my head. Ten years. That was how long I had known Vin. And for almost that whole time, we had been inseparable. We had gone to the same schools, were in the same classes all through elementary school and junior high. We spent long summer days and cold Christmas holidays together. Up until a few months ago, we hung out together after school almost every day. We liked the same kind of music, the same movies, the same video games. In ten years, you think you know a person. You think nothing they could do would ever surprise you.

"I never said anything about Robbie's watch," I said.

Vin's face sagged. He shook his head.

"You can either go to the cops yourself and tell them, or I will," I said.

A threat. Vin hated threats. They made him angry, made him fight back, made him try to get even. He straightened up. Some of the old Vin fire started to burn in his eyes.

"You're going to go to the cops about *me*?" he said. "They've already questioned you—what?—twice, three times. And now you're going to tell them you found Robbie Ducharme's watch in your locker and you think someone *else* put it there? You really think they're going to believe that, Mikey? You think if you tell them I put it there, I'm going to say, Yeah, I did it; I did something I didn't do?"

"*Did* you put Robbie's watch in my locker?" I said.

For a moment he just looked at me. He was still looking at me—looking me straight in the eyes—when he shook his head.

"But Cat asked me if I knew the combination," he said. "And I gave it to her. I didn't know what she was going to do, honest."

"But you knew the watch was there. You just said so."

"She told me. After the cops were here."

Probably like she told him, after, that she'd lied to the cops about seeing me with Robbie.

"But we're such good friends that you didn't tell me?" I said.

He looked down at the ground for a moment. When his eyes met mine again, I could tell he was sorry. He looked nervous and scared and sad, like something bad was going to happen and he was afraid what it might be and he wished he could go back in time and change it all.

"I wanted to tell you," he said. "I wanted to talk to you about it."

"But instead you let Cat set me up."

"She knew about you and your locker," he said. "Everyone knows your combination is no secret."

"So she decided, why not pin the blame on me?"

"No, Mikey—" Vin said.

"*No?* Jeez, Vin, do I look stupid?"

"I mean, no, she didn't think you'd actually get nailed for it. She said with your connections, you'd get a good lawyer."

By connections, he meant Riel.

"She said a good lawyer would say you didn't put Robbie Ducharme's watch in your locker, but that someone else did. Anyone could have put it in there, Mike, the way you hand out your locker combination. She said anything else the cops have, it's all circumstantial. She said by that time, though, the cops might never be able to figure out exactly what happened."

"And if I tell them what you just told me, that Cat put it there?"

"She'll just deny it."

"But you'll back me up, right?" I said. "Since you're my best friend."

He looked down at the ground again.

"You told Cat what I told you about Rebecca, too, didn't you?" I said. "Did you tell her to threaten Rebecca, too?"

Nothing. He didn't even look at me.

"Well, it didn't work," I said. "She was scared for a while." In fact, she'd been terrified for a while. "But she's not scared enough to stay quiet anymore. She's going to tell the cops that after she first talked to them, she did recognize one person coming out of the park that night. She's going to tell them about the threats she got too. The ones that made her afraid to go back and tell the cops more. Funny thing that she only got threatened after I told you about her. Her name was never in the paper. The cops never said who she was. You're the only person who knew, Vin."

"What about the person she saw coming out of the park? Maybe that person saw her too. Maybe that's who threatened her."

"Like I said, you're the *only* person who knew, Vin."

The color started to drain from his face. "Hey, come on, Mike."

"Come on, what? You let Cat try to hang Robbie Ducharme's death on me—you *help* her do it by giving her my locker combination—and now I'm supposed to feel sorry for you? Robbie's *dead*, Vin." I felt sick to my stomach having this conversation with him. "You were there. I know you were. Rebecca saw you. What happened? What did you do?"

Vin's face crunched up. I thought he was going to cry. "The guy was just such a geek, you know?"

"So you *killed* him?"

Vin's head swung up. His eyes were filled with fear. "No, it wasn't like that. We were in the park."

"We?"

"Me and A. J. and Cat and a bunch of the guys. We were just hanging out, you know, not bothering anyone. And along comes Robbie. A. J. just started to razz him a little. Then he asked Robbie for some money to buy cigarettes, and Robbie, jeez, instead of handing it over or even just walking on, Robbie starts in on why smoking is bad for you. Can you believe it? He tries to lecture

A. J. about smoking. And A. J. starts giving him an even harder time. Then some of the other guys started in. One of the guys blocked Robbie, so Robbie pushed him. The guy shoved him back. Then another guy shoved him and, I don't know, someone pushed him down and then . . . " He shook his head, his eyes glistening with unshed tears. "Then people just started kicking him."

People. I didn't have the stomach to ask if people included Vin. I didn't think I could stand to hear the answer.

"You have to go to the cops," I said again. "Because Rebecca is going to tell them everything she knows. And so am I."

I pulled the door open to go back into the school.

"Mike!"

I could have turned. I could have looked at Vin and listened to what he might tell me. But it wouldn't have changed what I had to do, so what was the point? I didn't turn back. Instead I went inside and headed down the hall. I hadn't gone far when I saw Riel coming out of the office with Ms. Rather and two cops. Coming out of the office and walking toward me.

CHAPTER ELEVEN

You'd think that when you had it all figured out, when you could finally prove that it wasn't you, that you *weren't* the one who had done it, then that would be that, you'd be in the clear—home free, no more worries. After all, that's the way it happens on TV, right?

Rebecca didn't go to school after I ran into her that morning. Instead she went to the cops, and she told them that she could identify one of the kids she had seen coming out of the park the night that Robbie Ducharme died. She told them that she hadn't come forward sooner because she was afraid. She told them that she had received two threatening phone calls. She told them exactly when she had received those calls. She even told them—and I wasn't sure how I felt about it, but it turns out Rebecca believes in the truth, the whole truth, and nothing but the truth—that she was a little afraid of me at first because she had seen me with Vin that day in the alley, and she assumed we were friends, and she thought maybe I had been there with him in the park. Then she'd seen me with him again right after she had talked to Riel, so she thought I must have told him she was the one. She told them, though, that she knew she had been wrong about me. But, she told them, she had *not* been wrong about Vin. After that, the cops came to school, looking for Vin.

I told the cops that I had found Robbie Ducharme's watch in my locker. I told them that I hadn't put it there. I told them—again—that I hadn't been in the park that night. I told them someone else put the watch into my locker and that the only person besides me who knew the combination to my lock was Vin. I told them if they didn't believe me, they could check with my best friend, Sal. I told them they could check with everyone who knew me, ask them to try to open my locker.

Then they wanted to talk about Robbie and me. So I told them—again—yeah, I got mad at him that one time when he said what he said about Billy. And yeah, I had pushed him; but I never meant to hurt him, and I was sorry it had happened. I told them that Cat—who, by the way, fellas, is Vin's girlfriend, and who, also by the way, was in the park with Vin that night—had seen me shove Robbie that first time and had probably made up the lie about me fighting with him the day before he died just to make me look bad. I told them I couldn't prove I hadn't done what she said, but there was no way she could prove I had. It was her word against mine.

That made me nervous because I didn't know what my word was worth anymore.

Finally, I told them—and, yes, I was embarrassed to admit it—that I had told Vin that it was Rebecca who had seen kids coming out of the park. I told them—and they already knew this—that Rebecca had been threatened for the first time *after* I told Vin that she was the person mentioned in the newspaper, the person who had seen kids in the park that night. I told them what Vin had told me about how it happened. I told them everything I knew. They wrote it all down. They said they would get back to me.

"Don't they believe me?" I said to Riel as we rode the elevator down to the ground floor of police headquarters.

"They have to check it all out," Riel said. "Maybe Vin's denying it."

"But he told me everything."

"*You* say he told you everything. Maybe *he* says you're making it all up."

I stared open-mouthed at him. "You don't believe me?"

Riel peered back at me. "I believe you, Mike," he said. "I always believed you."

"*Always?*"

He smiled, something that, now that I think about it, he doesn't do all that often. "I didn't say it was easy, but, yeah, *always*. Sometimes I think you try hard to buck it, Mike, but basically you're a good kid. You know right from wrong."

I'd lived with him long enough to know when he had finished what he'd been going to say and when he had just got started. So I waited.

"Next time, though," he said, "in fact, for the foreseeable future, it would be helpful if you'd tell me the truth."

I didn't think I was going to need much persuasion.

"I know this makes me seem like the loser of the century," I said, "but I really was following Jen. I just wanted to talk to her. And—" I hadn't exactly admitted this before. "I wanted to see what she was doing." I wasn't even sure what I thought she was up to. Maybe she was meeting a guy. Maybe she was doing something she shouldn't have been doing. Well, obviously she had been because, like me, she had lied about it to me, to her parents, and even to the police.

"They'll check everything out," Riel said. "I think it's going to be okay."

» » »

It took forever. For a couple of days it didn't seem like anything at all was going to happen. Then there was an article in the paper that said that an arrest had been made. It didn't say who it was—the identity of the person arrested wasn't made public because of his age. *His* age. But the rumor went around school pretty fast that it was A. J. Siropolous. The next day there was another article—four more arrests had been made. Three guys and one girl. I heard one of the guys was Vin. The girl was Cat. And then that was it for a while because these things take time—or so Riel told me. They take more time than you can imagine.

I felt sorry for Vin. He'd got himself caught up in something really bad. I felt sorry for Jen, too, but for a different reason.

The day after I talked to the cops we had an early closing at school. That happens every once in a while when the teachers have a staff meeting. Everyone gets out an hour early. I put that hour to good use. I took the bus uptown to Jen's school. I didn't go alone. I took a friend. And that friend was the one who waited at the gate to Jen's school, who picked Jen out of the crowd of kids flooding through that gate at three thirty, who talked to her and then brought her over to where I was waiting, out of sight, afraid that she wouldn't talk to me. Then my friend backed off, leaving me to talk to Jen.

Jen looked up at me for a few moments, searching my face with her green eyes. Then she said, "I'm glad everything's okay, Mike. I knew you weren't involved."

Well, thanks. "I couldn't have been involved, Jen," I said. "If I had been, I wouldn't have seen you down on Eastern Avenue that night. I wouldn't have seen you get into that car."

Some girls are tough, you know? You can call some girls the worst thing you can think of, you can break their hearts, you can disappoint them, you can be mean to them, and they'll never cry. Then there are girls like

Jen. Jen's eyes always seemed to be pooling up with tears, like they were now.

"I was wrong to follow you," I said. "I admit it. But, Jen? If it was the other way around, if you had seen me out doing something that maybe I wanted to keep a secret, but I was the only person in the world who could alibi you in something serious, like what happened to Robbie, I wouldn't have hesitated for a second." I had given it a lot of thought. I had tried to put myself in her shoes. I had tried to imagine what she could possibly have been doing that was worth trading my life for. I had tried to imagine what I could possibly ever find myself doing that would be worth trading *her* life for. And I couldn't come up with a single thing.

"I was with Peter," she whispered.

"Peter?"

"This guy I'm seeing." She wiped at her eyes. "I love him, Mike. But he's not in school. He's a musician. He's in a group. My parents don't like me seeing him. They're freaking out over him all the time. They think it's his fault my grades have slipped." For a moment she looked fierce. "I hate that school, Mike. I hate it all." She let out a long shivery sigh. "My parents took away my cell phone. If Peter calls the house, my mother says I'm not there. My dad insists on driving me everywhere—he thinks that way he can make me focus on my schoolwork and keep me away from Peter."

I remembered seeing her in her dad's car, her face serious, maybe even a little sad. I remembered her calling from a phone booth downtown. I remembered wondering why she didn't use her cell phone. I remembered, too, that when I had tried to call her cell, I got a No Service message. But, jeez—

"*That's* why you lied to the cops about where you were? Because you didn't want your parents to know you were meeting some guy?" Riel was right about people having their reasons for doing things—good or bad. But, jeez, was I supposed to give her the benefit of the doubt on *this?*

A tear ran down her cheek. "I knew you didn't have anything to do with it, Mike," she said. "But my parents were right there in the room with me."

"You could have asked to talk to the cops in private."

"Even if I had, and even if I'd told them where I was, they would have checked. They know you and I used to go together. If I said where I really was, they would have checked to make sure I wasn't lying to cover for you. They would have wanted to talk to Peter. And they would have talked to Ashley again and to her mother, and Ashley would have had to tell the truth. And my dad would have found out. My parents would never trust me again, Mike. Ever."

I stared at her. Jen. Someone I used to be crazy about. Had she changed so much since I'd known her, or had she been like this all along?

"They thought I was involved, Jen," I said. "They thought I was involved in *killing* Robbie Ducharme."

Her eyes glistened with tears. "But you weren't,"

she said. "And if you weren't, they'd have figured it out. They *did* figure it out. You didn't have to get *me* involved, Mike."

"Jeez, Jen, I came *this* close."

She started to blubber. "I'm sorry," she said. "I was wrong. I know I was wrong. If you want me to, I'll tell the police."

If I wanted her to. Like it was up to me. Like she had a choice. I waited for her to calm down a little. Then I said, "The cops are going to want to talk to you again, Jen. They're going to want to ask you again where you were. If you don't tell them about Peter this time, I'm going to have to. You understand that, right?"

She wiped her tears. Then she nodded.

"I know," she said. Her voice was soft, but solid now. Ready, maybe, to do the right thing. Ready to think about someone else for a change. Me. She looked over at my friend.

"Who's that?" she said. "Your new girlfriend?"

I glanced down the sidewalk where Rebecca was standing, waiting for me, her red hair ablaze in the afternoon sun.

"Maybe," I said.

After all, a guy can hope, right?

MORE MYSTERIES
FROM NORAH McCLINTOCK

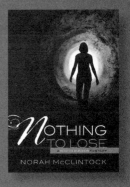

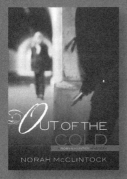

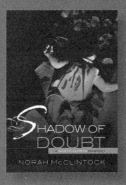

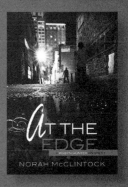

ABOUT THE AUTHOR

Norah McClintock is the author of several mystery series for teenagers and a five-time winner of the Crime Writers of Canada's Arthur Ellis Award for Best Juvenile Crime Novel. McClintock was born and raised in Montreal, Quebec. She lives in Toronto with her husband and children.